LIFE'S A WITCH

NEW ORLEANS

NOCTURNES

CARRIE PULKINEN

This is a work of fiction. Names, characters, places, and incidents are either the product of the author's imagination or are used fictitiously, and any resemblance to actual persons living or dead, business establishments, events, or locales, is entirely coincidental.

Life's a Witch

Contact Information: www.CarriePulkinen.com

Cover Art by Rebecca Poole of Dreams2Media
Edited by Krista Venero of Mountains Wanted

First Edition, 2020
ISBN: 978-1-7347624-0-2

Crimson Oliver is a bad witch.

She's not wicked, but every spell she tries to cast goes awry in one way or another. After her last screw-up, the high priestess has threatened to bind her powers and turn her human for good.

Crimson's solution? Challenge the priestess to a battle of magic she can't possibly win.

Not without a miracle, anyway.

Enter hotter-than-hellfire demon Mike Cortez. He's a devil's advocate who can make anyone's dreams come true…for a price. He's had his eye on the seductive witch for a while, and Satan is in the market for a new assistant.

But Mike wants to date her, not damn her.

When he accidentally makes a deal condemning Crimson to an eternity of satanic servitude, they'll have to go to hell and back to outsmart the devil and save the witch's soul.

Ride along on a journey from the Big Easy to the underworld and back again in this fast, steamy romantic comedy!

CHAPTER ONE

Crimson Oliver was a bad witch. Not bad as in wicked. She wasn't green—most witches weren't—and she didn't run around cackling at little girls, telling them she'd get them and their little dogs too.

She didn't ride a broom, and though she'd inquired about an army of flying monkeys, her request was ignored. No, Crimson didn't have a wicked bone in her body, but she was bad.

"Bad" as in nearly every spell she tried to cast went awry in some way or another, and that self-proclaimed "badness" was what had landed her in the hot seat in front of the entire Council of Elders in the New Orleans Coven of Witches.

Crimson sat in a straight-backed wooden chair, facing a long, rectangular table that occupied a two-foot-tall platform in the great room of a nineteenth-century mansion. Four elders flanked the high priestess perched in a burgundy velvet armchair at the center of the table. At five-foot-four with a stocky build, the priestess Rosemary wore her dark brown hair woven into long braids that cascaded down to her waist, and her eyes held contempt as she waited for the rest of the high-ranking witches in the coven to file into the room.

Tugging at the neck of her sweater, Crimson tried to alleviate the warmth her nerves were producing. It didn't help that the thermostat was set to eighty-five degrees.

She knew this trick. Every witch who'd ever screwed up knew Rosemary liked to turn up the heat—literally—just to watch the accused sweat.

What Crimson didn't know was why. Rosemary was the most powerful witch in the coven. Sure, her moral compass could have used some fine-tuning, but her position of high priestess granted her powers no other witch could achieve, no matter how much they practiced. Powers like the ability to bind another witch's magic, rendering her nothing more than human. She had everything a witch could want, so why did she take pleasure in tormenting her people?

Because she's a witch with a capital B. That's why.

As the last person entered the chamber, the door thudded shut, and Willow, a lanky blonde with icy blue eyes who sat to the left of the priestess, lifted her head. "Crimson Oliver, please stand."

Crimson turned her head slowly to the right and then the left before pressing her hand to her chest and mouthing the word *me?* She sat alone in the center of the room, for goddess' sake. It wasn't as if no one could tell who was being accused. The only reason they wanted her to stand was to increase the pressure, hoping she'd crack under the weighted gazes of all those high-ranking witches.

But Crimson was the queen of pressure. Her misfiring magic had landed her in enough sticky situations that she picked up everything but money and men. Pressure. *Ha!* She was like an Instant Pot on steroids when it came to pressure. She'd found herself in plenty of trouble more times than she could count, but she always found her way out of it. Well, almost always.

Willow blew out a hard breath through her nose. "Please stand so you may hear the charges brought against you."

"How will standing improve my hearing?"

The blonde witch's mouth fell open as she looked at the priestess, and Crimson rose to her feet. That was enough pushing back for now. She rested one hand on her hip and scanned the faces of her jury. Agatha's green eyes held concern, but Fern, the red-headed fauna witch, took resting bitch face to a whole new level.

Laila, the coven's second-in-command and advisor to the priestess, rose to her feet. Her curly black hair spilled over her shoulders, and sympathy filled her gaze as she locked eyes with Crimson. "Your charges are as follows: one, lying under oath when questioned about the disappearance of werewolf Jackson Altuve; two, reckless and intentionally harmful use of magic when you cast a spell you were unable to break; three, conspiring with the werewolves to cover up your misdeeds."

Laila pressed her lips together and shook her head. "If found guilty, the high priestess recommends the binding of your powers indefinitely. How do you plead?"

Crimson swallowed hard, lifting her chin in defiance to maintain her composure. "I'm innocent, of course."

The high priestess finally spoke, "Your boyfriend broke up with you, so you turned him into a cat. I'd hardly call that innocent."

That was *so* not how it happened. Crimson moved her other hand to her hip. "Did Jackson tell you that?"

"My information comes from his relative and was confirmed by the pack's alpha."

"Did they also tell you it was an accident? Because it was." Well, the actual turning him into a cat part was no accident. It had been part of a sex game they were playing: the wicked witch turns her familiar human and has her way with him. She turned Jax into a cat, easy peasy. The problem arose when she tried to change him into human form again.

Rosemary lifted one shoulder in a dismissive shrug. "Accident or no, you used your magic maliciously against another supe."

"I did no such thing."

Laila cleared her throat. "We've heard the accusations. Let's address them one at a time and give Crimson the opportunity to defend herself."

She crossed her arms. "Yes. Let's."

Rosemary clamped her mouth shut, nodding, and Laila continued, "Did you or did you not lie under oath about Jackson's disappearance?"

"I did not." Crimson lowered into the chair and crossed her legs. "The specific questions asked were whether or not I kidnapped Jackson or put a curse on his pack. I did neither of those things. Jackson stayed with me willingly for fear of ridicule if he returned to his pack in cat form. The so-called curse the questioning referred to involved the wolves being force-shifted at seemingly random times. I had no idea my attempts to change Jax back into his human form were affecting the other wolves, so no, I didn't lie about either of those things."

Laila nodded. "The Council has reviewed the questions and answers provided. I move to dismiss the charge of lying under oath. All those in favor?"

Everyone on the platform raised their hand, except Rosemary, of course, who made being in the coven feel like living inside the movie *Mean Girls*. Crimson suppressed a smile as she imagined dragging her chair up to the platform just so the priestess would say, "You can't sit with us."

"Moving on to charge number two: reckless and intentionally harmful use of magic." Laila scanned the paper on the table. "Did you or did you not turn the werewolf into a cat when he threatened to break up with you?"

"No." Crimson clenched her teeth. If she was going to get out of this with her magic intact, she'd have to throw Jax under the bus. Sure, he might be humiliated when the truth came out, but it was better than being turned human.

"So you *didn't* turn Jackson Altuve into a cat?"

"Oh, I did, but he agreed to it."

Fern's brows disappeared into her bangs, and Agatha's eyes widened.

Sorry, Jax. There's no way around it. Anyway, he said he'd call her, but he never did. Served him right. "It was a sex game."

Snickering sounded from the witches behind her, and Willow's cheeks turned pink. As Crimson explained what happened, the murmur in the audience grew louder. She twisted in her chair to stare daggers at the people making fun of her. "If you find it that amusing, I can't imagine how boring your sex lives must be."

Mouths fell open, and several people gasped. Crimson smirked and turned her attention back to Laila. "Intentionally harmful? Absolutely not. Reckless?" She cast her gaze to the ceiling for a moment and pursed her lips. "Not reckless, either. We planned it. The spell went wrong, that's all." It happened all the time. Crimson was bad at being a witch, but that was her lot in life, and she'd rather build on it than leave it empty.

Rosemary slapped her palm on the table. "And that was your third strike."

"I fixed it, so it doesn't count."

"It does."

"Let's move on to the final charge." Laila's soothing voice broke the tension. "Did you conspire with the were-wolves to cover up your misdeed? A Sophie Burroughs to be specific?"

"Sophie wasn't a werewolf when I discussed the situation with her. She didn't become one until the entire ordeal ended." Thank the goddess they didn't ask about her boyfriend, Trace. He actually *was* a werewolf at the time. "In fact, Sophie was a witch with bound powers. If this coven were the welcoming place it used to be, we might have been able to help her."

The priestess narrowed her eyes. "You can skirt around the edges of these accusations all you want. It doesn't change the fact that you're an incompetent witch who's a danger to herself and others. You've already shrunk a politician's penis to the size of a Vienna sausage and made a priest speak all his thoughts aloud. Now you've almost caused a war between the witches and the werewolves. We can't risk you having powers."

Laila came to her defense. "She did remedy the situation without the help of the council this time. I vote she gets one more chance."

The other witches nodded their agreement, and Rose-mary's face pinched. "Without the help of the council, maybe, but not without the help of another witch. A dead one."

The whispering behind her grew into a murmur, and Crimson shot to her feet. "It's true. I needed to channel the magic of a fauna witch, so I convinced a necromancer to summon the spirit of a powerful one. With her assistance, I solved the problem without inconveniencing the coven in the slightest."

Rosemary stood, leaning her hands on the table and looming her authority over the coven. "We almost went to war for your incompetence."

"You'd love a war. You get off on all this power; everyone can see that. You're high priestess over a coven that cowers beneath your rule."

Straightening, Rosemary clasped her hands and nodded slowly. "Your inability to break the spell on your own is a symbol of your ineptitude. As high priestess of this coven, I demand your powers be bound at once." She cast her gaze to the witches on her right, then her left. "Does anyone oppose?"

Laila inhaled as if she were about to come to Crimson's defense, but much like Gretchen Weiners, the second-ranking Mean Girl in the clique, she kept her mouth shut to avoid being pounded by the bully.

Crimson's heart plopped into her stomach like a Mentos into a bottle of Diet Coke, and she swallowed the bitterness creeping up the back of her throat. "You can't be serious. No one opposes this?"

Every member of the council—aside from the Queen Bee, of course—cast her gaze to the table or the ceiling, refusing to make eye contact.

"You don't belong here." Rosemary motioned toward

an intern standing by the wall. "Bring the grimoire. The binding will happen immediately."

"This isn't a high school clique." Crimson's voice pitched in panic. "It's a coven, and I'm a witch—I belong."

A young woman laid a thick volume on the table, and Laila rested her hand on the wooden cover. "The binding spell in this book is permanent." She looked at Rosemary. "Are you sure you want to do this to her?"

The priestess sneered. "Absolutely positive. It's past time a threat like her was neutralized."

A threat? Seriously, what did this woman have against her? Rosemary had always been a snob, but the moment she was elected high priestess, she'd made it her mission to make Crimson's life miserable. Crimson could admit she wasn't the best at casting spells. On her deathbed, her mother had unbound all of her magic in a rush. Crimson was just a child, and something had gone wrong. It was the only explanation for her skewed magic, and it wasn't her fault.

The other witches took pity on Crimson, which annoyed the hell out of her, but Rosemary treated her like a mangy mutt who wouldn't get off her doorstep.

"Let's see. Where is that spell? Oh, here it is." The priestess tugged on a ribbon and opened the book to the exact page.

"You had it bookmarked?" Crimson gasped.

Rosemary knew. She *knew* she'd find a way to force the council to agree with her—to at least not oppose her. She always did. The coven trembled in fear with Rosemary as their leader, and her reign of terror needed to end.

Fisting her hands at her sides, Crimson stood and summoned her courage—or maybe her stupidity—the jury was still out on that one—and sent her words up in prayer. "In the name of the goddess Morrigan, I denounce your authority and hereby invoke the Supremacy Challenge Law."

Rosemary scoffed. "You can't do that. You're on trial."

Crimson lifted her chin defiantly and pressed her palms together. "Morrigan, goddess of battle and sovereignty, with your blessing, I call for the Supremacy Challenge to be granted."

The lights flickered, the energy in the room growing electric as a silence descended so deafening you could have heard a leprechaun scratch his ass. Crimson's arm hairs stood on end, and no one dared utter a breath as the goddess' decision charged the air.

In unison, every mouth in the room opened and said, "So mote it be." A collective gasp followed the proclamation, and Crimson's head spun like she was on a merry-go-round at top speed.

What had she done?

Rosemary stared blankly ahead, her eyes wide as hula hoops, no doubt in just as much shock as Crimson that the goddess granted her request. A Supremacy Challenge hadn't been issued in the past hundred years, and now Crimson of all people was to go up against the high priestess in a battle of magical skill?

What the hell was she thinking?

This pairing was like a chihuahua versus a pit bull. It didn't matter how much fight Crimson had in her, Rosemary would chew her up and spit her out like a stick of Fruit Stripe gum.

Laila took the grimoire and turned to a page in the back. "When the goddess grants a Supremacy Challenge request, the two witches will go head-to-head in a battle of magic. The winner will be high priestess of the coven, while the loser will have her powers bound for life and be exiled from the city, never to associate with another witch again. According to tradition, you have one month to prepare for the challenge." She looked at Crimson. "And you can't channel another witch's magic to win."

"I suggest you keep your head down for the next thirty days." Rosemary stood. "Your witching days are over. This meeting is adjourned."

As the witches filed out of the great room, Crimson sank into her chair, chewing the inside of her cheek and stewing over her predicament. What in the goddess' name did she think would happen when she called for a challenge like that?

Well, for one, she didn't think the goddess would actually grant it. And channeling was her inborn gift. How was she to know she wouldn't be allowed to use the only magic that consistently worked for her? Not that it would matter. She'd need to channel the goddess herself to win this, which she *should* have been able to do if her magic hadn't glitched when her mother unbound it.

If this wasn't incentive to hit the books and study, she didn't know what was. Her spells worked sometimes. She'd just have to make sure those sometimes happened during the challenge.

Everyone in the coven agreed Rosemary was a ruthless bitch, and Crimson suspected that, secretly, they'd all love to see her removed from power. There had been peace among the supes of New Orleans for decades, yet she ruled like they were always on the verge of war. And the way she treated Crimson, singling her out the way she did, didn't make any sense at all.

A low-level witch whose spells went haywire more often than they worked wasn't a threat, yet the high priestess acted like she was. There had to be more to this vendetta than mean girl behavior.

Crimson rose to her feet and strutted toward the table. "Why do you hate me? Aside from my magic not working correctly, I've never done a damn thing to warrant this treatment from you."

Defensiveness flickered in Rosemary's eyes before she straightened her spine. "I don't want incompetence in my ranks. Nothing more. I only wanted to turn you human. Now that you've challenged me, I'm going to squash you like the dung beetle you are."

If I'm a dung beetle, then you're a piece of dung. Turning on her heel, Crimson strode out the door. She could smell bullshit a mile away, and the high priestess reeked of manure. There was a reason Rosemary wanted her without magical powers, and she planned to find out why.

But first, she had to devise a way to out-magic the most powerful witch in New Orleans.

CHAPTER TWO

Mike Cortez bit the inside of his cheek and forced himself to enter the meeting room at the Priscilla St. James Community Center. A registration table sat to the left, and he stopped to sign in, scribbling his name on a paper nametag and sticking it to his shirt—a ridiculous requirement, seeing as how he'd known everyone in the room for at least fifty years.

He passed the beverage station, inhaling the rich, earthy aroma of the world's worst coffee—seriously, it smelled divine, but that shit tasted like it came straight from the tarpits of hell—and dropped his food contribution, a box of mini angel food cakes from Sweet Destiny's Bakery, onto the snack table.

As soon as the package hit the surface, the other demons in the room swarmed it, shoving the pastries into their mouths and moaning as if they were better than sex with Aphrodite. For a full-blooded recovering demon, he supposed they were.

Sweet Destiny, the bakery next door to Mike's restaurant, was owned by an angel named Destiny Monroe. She baked a little extra magic into his weekly order for the Hellions Anonymous meetings, as it helped to curb his friends' demonic nature, at least for a little while.

"Thanks, Mike," Richard said, his mouth full of angelic cake. "If you weren't still Satan's bitch, I'd kiss you."

A famine demon back in the day, Richard used to appear as nothing more than skin stretched over a skeleton as he poisoned crops and spread drought throughout the lands. His work on the Irish potato famine had secured his release from the Devil's clutches, and he'd been a glutton ever since. Now, his potbelly hung over his belt so far Mike doubted the man had seen his own dick in decades.

"No worries," Mike grumbled. One perk of having a handshake from hell—no other recovering demon would touch him for fear of being sucked back into the under-world. Of course, they all knew his power didn't work that way, but no one wanted to take any chances.

Mike sank into a chair in the "Circle of Hope" and crossed his arms, tucking his fisted right hand beneath his pit. His palm itched, the first signal he was late on his payment to Satan. If he didn't make a deal on the Devil's behalf soon, his ass would be grass, and not the fun kind you could smoke.

"Good evening, everyone." Katrina crossed one long, slender leg over the other, lacing her fingers and resting them on her bare knee. That was all it took for the former succubus to command the room's attention. Her long brown hair cascaded over her shoulders in thick waves, and dark lashes fringed her striking lavender eyes.

A bit of drool rolled from the corner of Richard's mouth, and Sarah bit her bottom lip as she twirled a lock of blonde hair around her finger. Blood began to pool in

Mike's groin, and he shifted uncomfortably in his chair. If the Hellions Anonymous leader didn't get her magic in check, this meeting would turn into an orgy faster than roux could scorch on an unattended stove.

He cleared his throat. "Katrina, your demon is showing."

Her eyes flashed red as she raked her gaze up and down his body. "You're not showing nearly enough."

Sarah rubbed a hand along her thigh, gripping her jeans as if to stop herself from rubbing another area. "Someone get this woman a piece of cake before we all end up naked."

Mike strode to the snack table but found the box empty. "Richard…" For fuck's sake, did the man have no control?

"Sorry," Richard said around a mouthful of cake. His plate held four more pieces, so he tossed one to Katrina.

She bit into the pastry, and an erotic moan emanated from her throat, electrifying the energy in the room. Mike held his breath as she finished the angelic cake, willing his dick to retreat. Succubi could get an entire crowd hot and horny with a snap of their fingers, and no one—not even Satan himself—was immune to their powers. It had been years since he'd seen Katrina without her glamour on, and the fact she'd dropped it tonight could only mean one thing: she'd gotten laid.

"My apologies." With a deep inhale, she activated her concealing magic, transforming her appearance from hottest stripper in New Orleans to Karen the soccer mom. "After seventeen years of celibacy, I had a moment of weakness last night. It seems I'm still not free from Satan's clutches."

"It's okay," Sarah said. "Your time will come."

Katrina grinned devilishly. "My date sure came. Again and again. I'm afraid I've ruined him for other women." She straightened her spine. "But I'm back on the wagon. No more sex until Satan releases me. I will abstain until he gives up on me."

"You know that's not how the Devil works." Mike rubbed his palm on his jeans, the mere thought of striking a deal making it burn. "No one is free from the bowels of hell unless they pay a price or win a bet."

She made a noncommittal sound and smirked at him before addressing the group. "Hi, my name is Katrina, and I'm a succubus."

"Hi, Katrina," the demons said in unison.

"I was banned from hell when Satan's flavor of the month found us in a compromising position in his chambers. After living topside for one hundred fifty years, I've grown fond of humans and refuse to use my sexuality as a tool to send their souls to the underworld. The devil *will* forget about me eventually, and my demonic desires will cease, at which time I'll be free to find love and live a normal life."

It'll never happen, Mike wanted to say, but he held his tongue. The Devil never forgot, but if she believed she had the stamina to give Satan a run for his money, more power to her.

They went around the circle, introducing themselves, telling their stories of how they won their freedom and mentioning any slip-ups they may have had between meetings. It was the same damn routine every week, but HA meetings were required—as part of the truce with the humans—of every recovering demon who called New Orleans home.

Most of the demons there had struck a deal with the

Devil to earn their release. Sarah, a pestilence demon, bargained for her freedom and won release when she initiated the bubonic plague by sneezing on a bartender in London. Mark planted the seed that started World War II, and Denise was especially proud of herself for instigating the #metoo phenomenon that rocked Hollywood, knocking a slew of famous actors and directors off their pedestals. She outsmarted Satan on that one. Sure, it caused all the turmoil he was hoping for, but it also brought to light a persistent problem as women all over the country found solidarity in the movement.

The Devil wasn't happy about the good that came from Denise's "evil" deed, but the bargain had already been struck, and Satan never reneged on a deal.

Mike tapped his foot, fisting his hand until his nails dug into his palm. He should have been out there looking for a morally inept idiot to bargain with, not sitting in this boring room with its off-white walls and matching tile floor, the smell of coffee barely masking the stench of mildew growing on the window panes. He had a restaurant to run, a life to live, and he'd never been this late giving the Devil his due.

"Mike?" Sarah waved a hand in front of his face, pulling him out of his thoughts and into the meeting. "It's your turn."

"Right. I'm Mike, and I—"

"Hi, Mike," everyone said.

He ground his teeth. "I'm a Devil's advocate, and I won partial freedom in a poker game with Satan five years ago. As long as I make a deal for him once a month, I get to live topside, left to my own devices, but I'm two weeks late, so I've got to jet early." The burning sensation in his palm engulfed his entire hand.

"You should stay." Katrina folded her hands in her lap. "Show Satan he can't control you. Refuse to do his bidding."

"It doesn't work that way." He stood and stepped behind his chair. "A deal a month or I'm back in hell, never allowed to see the light of day again."

"You could hide," Richard said.

Mike shook his head. "Advocates can't hide. We make deals on behalf of Satan, so we're connected. I've explained all this before, and I don't have time to do it again. I've signed in and introduced myself, so I met the requirement. I'll see you next week."

He turned and strode out the door, stalking down the sidewalk toward Magazine Street. Though demons in hell were known for lying, cheating, stealing, and causing as much chaos as possible, those that lived topside strived to assimilate to the positive aspects of human nature. Mike wasn't lying when he said he had a connection to Satan. All advocates did, but while the Devil refused to sever the connection when Mike won the poker game, he did promise not to use it unless there was an emergency.

Now, as Mike passed the grand colonial homes of the Garden District, with their white columns and manicured lawns, a buzzing in his blood reminded him that connection was alive and well. Satan was calling, and Mike had no choice but to answer.

He slowed his pace as he passed a group of men congregating outside a bar. A tall brunet leaned against the blue wooden exterior, clutching his phone, while a short, stocky guy sipped his beer and shook his head. Eavesdropping on their conversation, Mike learned the tall one had recently been dumped and wasn't handling the breakup well.

Scorned lovers were easy targets, and Mike could have joined the conversation, steering it toward what the man would be willing to give up in exchange for another chance with his girl. But as he focused his magic, peering into their auras and breathing in their scents, not a single one of them reeked of malice; no evil danced in the energy around them.

He couldn't bring himself to curse an innocent. In the five years since he'd won his right to live among mortals, he'd made certain to target only wicked people when he made his monthly payments. He continued on his way.

"Voicemail again." The guy shoved his phone into his pocket. "Fuck that bitch. She'll be sorry she ever dumped me when I'm through."

Mike halted in his tracks, the malicious statement piquing his demonic interest. Perhaps he'd missed something in this guy's aura. He strolled toward the spurned human and placed a hand on his shoulder, activating his magic and willing the man to reveal his innermost desire. "What do you really want?"

The human's eyes blanked for a moment before filling with tears. "To talk to her."

"What would you be willing to trade?"

He tilted his head, giving Mike a curious look. "I'd give my left nut if she'd just pick up the phone."

Mike's palm turned red with the need to seal that deal. A man could function with only one testicle. Sure, the removal process wouldn't be pleasant, but that wasn't Mike's job. He just had to get a little bit of blood and a handshake, and he'd be good to go until the next payment was due.

A low growl rumbled in his chest as he remembered Satan's last email. *No more testicles.* His collection already filled two chambers in his halls, and his current girlfriend insisted he not add another nut unless he had the dick to match.

"It's time to move on." He patted the guy's back and continued down the sidewalk.

The buzzing in his blood grew stronger as he stalked toward his restaurant. Situated in a nineteenth-century Victorian home with a blue and white façade and an expansive front porch, Honoré's served the best fried oyster po-boy in town. Their red beans and rice were a favorite among the locals, and it put them on the map as a popular stop for foodie tours in the area.

Wiping the scowl from his face, he nodded a hello to his manager before making his way through the dining area toward the kitchen. He caught bits and pieces of conversations as he passed the patrons, but no one sounded desperate enough to need the Devil's help. Pausing at the kitchen entrance, he turned and scanned the auras of his customers, not finding a single wicked soul in the building, aside from his own.

He shook his head and marched through the kitchen. Was it too much to ask to get a truly evil person to pass through his restaurant every now and then? Once a month would be nice, but he'd settle for a few times a year. It would make his life a helluva lot easier.

Stepping into his office, he slammed the door and leaned against the wall, not bothering to turn on the lights because demons could see just fine in the dark. Squeezing his eyes shut, he pinched the bridge of his nose as the humming in his blood grew stronger. What the hell was he going to do? "Satan's balls," he grumbled.

"They're hanging a little to the left today. Thanks for asking."

Shit. Mike opened his eyes as the high-backed leather office chair spun around, with the Devil himself perched on the seat like a James Bond villain. He wore a pinstriped suit in a shade of red so dark it was almost black, with a blood-red tie and matching handkerchief in his breast pocket. He had enough gel in his jet-black hair to hold it still in a hurricane. Thick brows peaked above eyes the color of molten lava, the liquid shades of red undulating like a storm in his irises. The only thing missing from the movie-like scene was a cat for him to stroke in his lap. Then again, Satan was more of a hellhound man.

Mike bit his tongue, holding in the urge to ask the Devil if he'd seen any good spy movies lately. Satan hated being compared to Hollywood stereotypes of wicked men. Pushing from the wall, Mike dipped his head in a bow. "To what do I owe the honor, oh Great Evil One?"

Satan chuckled. "You don't look the slightest bit surprised to see me, Michael."

Surprised? Not hardly. Disappointed, disgusted, and dismayed? All of the above. "I felt your impending approach."

The Devil propped an ankle on his knee and drummed his fingers together. "Ah, yes, that's right. We're still connected because *I own you.*"

"Thanks for the reminder." Cutting the pretense, he dropped into the vinyl chair across from the desk. "I know I'm late on my payment, but I'll have a deal made by the end of the day tomorrow." *Even if it kills me.*

Satan cocked his head. "Are you late? I hadn't noticed."

Mike's eyes widened. *Oh, shit.* "If you aren't here to collect…"

"Do you think I'd bother coming all the way topside for the simple issue of a late payment? I'd send one of my guards to collect." He leaned forward. "I have a job for you."

Mike lifted his hands, leaning back in the chair, away from Satan. "Oh, no. No more jobs. I won this sorry excuse for freedom fair and square. You can't default on your contracts."

"You used to be my favorite advocate." He swiveled the chair from side to side, examining his nails before rubbing them on his lapel. "Your half-human nature made you the perfect tool for securing souls and whatever else I've felt like collecting over the years."

He stopped swiveling and leaned his forearms on the desk. "I've moved on from testicles to dignity now. Did I tell you that? Extreme, life-altering humiliation in exchange for whatever frivolous thing the human thinks he needs. It's quite fun."

"Sounds like a blast."

"Anyway, I've run into a dilemma, and I need you to find a new witch to be my assistant. I'm afraid my girl-friend wasn't fond of my old one. My little pookykins is the jealous type—most banshees are. She was sentenced to eternal damnation for grinding her cheating husband's sausage to bits, and I just can't get enough of her."

Mike fought his eye roll. "You know I can't damn a witch, sir. There's a truce among the supes here. We all play nice and keep the balance, and everyone gets to live in peace."

Satan sucked in a breath through his teeth, grimacing like it pained him to make the request. "You know I've never cared for playing nice. Keeping the balance is impor-tant, but that's an angels and demons affair. Witches have nothing to do with it." He shrugged. "I need a witch, and you're going to get her for me. It's the last job I'll ask of you. I swear."

Mike held in a groan. "I mean no disrespect, sir, but my contract states that as long as I pay my monthly fee, I'm a free demon. I don't have to take on additional jobs." Why did he feel like he was negotiating with a mob boss rather than Satan?

"You make a good point, and I appreciate a demon who has the balls to stand up to me. Yours would make a nice addition to my collection. I wonder…" He shook his head. "I digress. What was I saying? Oh, yes. I want to make you a deal." Satan stood and paced around the desk.

"Let me guess. It'll be an offer I can't refuse?"

"I don't think you'll want to refuse this. You're two weeks late on payment. Since we never discussed a grace period, I assert that there isn't one. It's my right to take you back to hell with me immediately."

His stomach sank, attempting to take his entire body with it, but he held his spine rigid, refusing to cower before the leader of the underworld.

"I could make *you* my personal assistant. Now there's a thought." He crossed his arms and seemed to drift inward for a moment. "No, witches' powers make them much more efficient and valuable. My assistant has always been a witch, and I want a new one. Here's my offer."

Satan's molten eyes churned with his magic. "Get me a witch by month's end, a truly wicked one—they're much more fun—and I'll dissolve your contract. No more payments. No more direct line to the ruler of hell. You'll be free."

The Devil was right. He didn't want to refuse. There were plenty of wicked witches in the world. He'd find one who danced on the darker side of magic. Hell, he might be able to convince one to join Satan of her own free will. Personal Assistant to the Prince of the Underworld could be an enticing title to a powerful being with questionable morals.

But he'd be violating the truce. Sure, he may win his freedom, but upsetting the supernatural balance in the most magical city in the country would be detrimental. He'd be banished or vanquished. It might even start a war.

He closed his eyes for a long blink, his jaw ticking as he ground his teeth. "And if I don't?"

Satan lit a fireball in his palm, toying with it as a menacing chuckle rose from his chest. "You'll return to hell, and I'll burn your precious restaurant to the ground, with all your patrons inside it." He tossed the fire into a trash can, and with a wave of his hand, he opened a portal and stepped through it.

Mike groaned. "Fuck me."

The Devil's head appeared through the shrinking portal. "You should have made that offer *before* I met my pookykins." With a wink, he disappeared, and the portal closed completely.

CHAPTER THREE

"Are you sure you want to hang out here tonight?" Sophie touched Crimson's elbow, pausing outside The Tipsy Leprechaun. Her long blonde hair hung in loose waves over her shoulders, and her blue eyes held concern. "This is such a popular place for supes. There'll probably be some of your coven sisters here. Maybe we should go to a human bar."

Crimson glanced at the entrance. The black door blended in with the black wood slats in the wall, making it almost unnoticeable. From Frenchman Street, the space looked like it belonged to the jazz club next door. The windows were blacked out and the main door locked to discourage humans from coming in. Supes knew the entrance lay around the corner in the alley, and this was one of the few places they could hang out together and let their guards down.

Not that humans weren't allowed. They were, but there was usually so much magic mixing in the air inside, it would give the mundane a killer case of the heebie-jeebies, and they'd leave on their own.

"I've only got a month left of being a supe myself, so I better make the most of it." Crimson tugged on the hem of her royal blue sweater.

"Don't talk like that. You're going to win that challenge with so many flying colors they'll think you've turned into a unicorn."

"As long as I don't fart glitter and puke rainbows."

Sophie's mouth formed an O shape. "I have so much to learn about supes."

Crimson pressed her lips into a line, fighting a smile.

"Oh, you're joking." She stuck out her tongue. "Haha. Pick on the newbie. That never gets old."

Crimson laughed. "Actually, I've never seen a unicorn. Maybe they do fart glitter. Who knows?"

"Shall we?" Sophie gestured to the door.

"Yep. I hope some witches are here. They need to see I won't be intimidated by a bully who acts like she's queen bee of the high school lunchroom." Straightening her spine, she brushed her curls behind her shoulders and stepped through the door.

A bar lined the wall to the right, with colorful glass bottles holding every kind of libation imaginable filling the shelves. To the left, a stage behind the small dance floor held a five-piece band belting out Frank Sinatra covers, and tables dotted the rest of the room.

"There's an empty one over there." Sophie pointed to a spot near the dance floor.

As they made their way toward it, the hottest demon this side of hell approached, his dark brown eyes flashing red as a devilish smile curved his full lips. Crimson's stomach fluttered as she took in all six-feet-four inches of his solid, muscular frame. Even with her heels on, he was taller than her, and that tipped the sexiness scale in his favor. Not that he needed any help.

With dark, wavy hair, a light brown complexion, and strong, masculine features, Mike Cortez looked like sin on a stick. Exactly the type of man she needed to stay away from.

Holding a glass of whiskey in one hand, he stopped in front of them and took a sip, his eyes locking with hers. "A witch and a werewolf walk into a bar. There's a punchline in there somewhere."

"And they walk right past a demon." Crimson held his gaze—and her breath—as she stepped around him. The signals in her brain went haywire, part of her wanting to run as fast as she could, and the other part wanting to grab him by the shoulders and find out if sin tasted as good as it looked. *Damn him.* Oh, wait. He was a demon. He was already damned.

He chuckled and turned to Sophie. "How's canine life treating you? You left the old man at home tonight?"

"Hi, Mike. It's good to see you." Sophie gave him a quick hug while Crimson inched farther away from the temptation. "Trace is hunting with Jax tonight. I can't wait 'til he gets home, though. Being a werewolf has worked wonders for my sex drive. We fuck like rabbits." Her eyes widened, and she covered her mouth. "I did not mean to say that out loud."

"Well, tell him I said hello, and have fun tonight. I'll see you ladies later." He winked at Crimson and disappeared into the crowd.

"I have got to learn to watch my mouth." Sophie slid into a chair, and Crimson sat next to her. "You were acting weird. I'm no empath, but I think I detected some sexual tension between you two. Have you done it with a demon?"

Crimson laughed. "I wish." Well, part of her did anyway.

"With the way he looked at you, he seemed willing to grant. Do y'all have history?"

"I met him at a New Year's Eve party. All he had to do was look at me, and he set off enough fireworks to put the city's display to shame." Her lips tugged into a smile as she recalled the night. "We danced a bit and talked a lot. Then he asked me how I wanted to start out the new year, and I told him preferably bent over a table with him taking me from behind. I was mortified to say the least."

Sophie giggled. "But you *were* thinking it."

"Who wouldn't be? Anyway, I ducked out before midnight to wallow in my humility and vowed to never drink enough to run my mouth like that again."

"Have you talked to him since?"

"I see him every now and then. I suppose you could call us casual acquaintances."

"Who have casual sex?" She wiggled her brows.

Crimson inhaled deeply as her gaze landed on Mike's backside while he leaned his elbows on the bar. How could someone so bad look so good? "Absolutely not. Don't get me wrong, the man is gorgeous."

Sophie nodded. "He's a panty-dropper for sure."

"But he's a *demon*. They're always up to no good."

"I don't know. Trace said he was a great guy and that he left hell for a reason. I assume that reason is because he's not actually evil." She shrugged. "I hear there's a support group for recovering demons, kinda like AA. I wonder if he goes."

"It doesn't matter if he does. My dad is an Earth-bound angel, and he always warned me to stay away from demons because, recovering or not, they're trouble. I'm in enough hot water as it is. I don't need to invite the devil into my bed, no matter how hot the sex might be."

Sophie gripped her forearm. "Wait. You're half angel? Why did I not know this?"

"My adoptive father is the angel. The biological one was human as far as I know."

"You never met him?"

She shook her head. "You know the saying 'What happens in Vegas stays in Vegas'?"

Sophie arched a brow. "Yeah."

"Well, for my mom, what happened in Vegas is now a twenty-six year old witch who's about to be turned human if she can't get her shit straight." She lifted a hand to flag down the waitress and ordered a vodka sour. "Make it a double, please."

"I'll have a glass of chardonnay," Sophie said. She waited for the waitress to walk away before placing her hand on top of Crimson's. "If you need a volunteer to cast your challenge spells on, you know you can count on me."

"I couldn't ask you to do that."

"Why not? I did it for Jane. She glamoured and bit me in front of the entire vampire council. First time she'd ever drunk blood from the source. You can turn me into a cat for a few minutes or whatever else you need to do."

Crimson rubbed her forehead. "What if I can't change you back?"

"You've got my grandma's spell. I know you can do it."

"That spell required the help of a fauna witch, remember? I'm not allowed to channel another witch's magic."

"You've got a month. You'll figure it out." Something caught Sophie's gaze, and she narrowed her eyes.

"Speaking of witches, are those friends of yours?" She nodded toward a table in the corner.

Crimson turned, and sure enough, Fern, Laila, and three other witches were chatting over drinks. She scanned the rest of the bar, but priestess Rosemary was nowhere around. "Do you mind if I go talk to them for a minute?"

The waitress delivered their drinks, and Sophie took a sip of wine. "Sure. I'll keep an eye on your demon for you."

"He's not my demon."

"He could be. Even if it's just for a couple of hours, he'd be a nice distraction."

"I'm sure he'd be a fantastic one." She was already in trouble up to her eyeballs. How much worse could it get? Crimson picked up her glass, sneaking one more glance at Mike's delicious backside—she might just consider Sophie's suggestion—before strutting toward the witches. "Hello, ladies."

The group quieted, their postures stiffening with unease as Crimson sank into an empty chair. She plastered on her most confident smile and looked each one of them in the eyes.

Laila, the only witch who didn't act like Crimson had the plague, smiled warmly. "How are you?"

She sucked down half her vodka sour in one gulp. "Aside from being granted a challenge I never expected to receive? Never better."

"Why did you make that request?" Laila asked. "And to call on the goddess in the form of Morrigan… What were you thinking?"

"I panicked. Morrigan was the first name I thought of to help, and…" She shrugged. "C'mon, you'd all love to see Rosemary dethroned. Admit it."

Fern shifted in her seat uncomfortably, and the others refused to make eye contact.

Crimson drummed her nails on the table. "I'm curious. Did y'all actually vote for Rosemary to be high priestess? I seem to remember her not being very well-liked in the coven before she was elected."

"She ran unopposed," Luna, a soft-spoken witch with short brown hair said, her eyes cast to the table.

"I wonder why that is." Crimson downed the rest of her drink, not expecting an answer.

Luna finally looked at her. "I heard she threatened to ruin anyone who ran against her."

Fern cleared her throat. "I heard that too."

Sounds like Rosemary. "Fern, I can't channel another witch's magic, but it doesn't say I can't have an assistant. Will you help me?"

Fern swallowed hard.

"I was thinking, since you're a fauna witch, maybe you could work with me? Stand with me during the challenge and give me some guidance if I start to do something wrong. I struggle with animal spells the most, I think."

"Uh…" Fern's eyes widened, and she cut her gaze between Laila and Crimson as she stuttered.

"Unfortunately, that won't fly," Laila said. "You can have assistance in your preparation, but the actual challenge is one witch against the other. No help allowed."

"Damn."

Fern's shoulders relaxed, and she sipped her daiquiri. "Sorry, Crim."

"Well, would you mind going over some spells with me ahead of time? Maybe you can help me figure out where I go wrong when I screw them up?"

"I would, but I really don't want to get on Rosemary's bad side."

"No one does," Laila said. "That's why she ran for high priestess unopposed."

"You would make an amazing high priestess, Laila," Luna said. "If Rosemary ever retires, you should run."

Laila shook her head "I'm meant to be an advisor, not high priestess. We have several members who are powerful enough to take Rosemary's place when she steps down."

Fern laughed. "That'll never happen. Someone will have to drop a house on that wicked witch before she'll give up power."

Now there was an idea… Crimson cast a glance toward Mike. Just how bad of a demon was he? She didn't have a clue what kind of magic he possessed, but he had to lack morals. All demons did. *Don't be ridiculous, Crim. You got yourself into this mess, and no amount of wishful heel-clicking is going to get you out.* It was a nice fantasy, though.

"Y'all talk like I don't have a chance of winning this."

No one responded.

"Well, if any of you can clue me in as to why our beloved high priestess has singled me out for her bitchery, I'm all ears." Still no one responded, so she set her glass on the table and stood. "No worries. I'll put her in her place after I beat her in the challenge."

"That'll take a miracle," Fern laughed.

Crimson turned on her heel and made a beeline for the restroom. *After I beat her in the challenge.* Now, that was funny. At least she'd sounded like she meant it. Confidence was key.

She brushed a dark curl from her forehead and stared at her reflection in the mirror. It *would* take a miracle for her to make it through with her magic intact, and she had a direct connection with the miracle department. Well, it wasn't exactly direct. She'd have to go through her dad, but he was a reasonable man. His assignment of watching over her as a child may have ended, but he loved her as if she were his own flesh and blood. She'd call him first thing tomorrow.

The bathroom door swung open, and Laila hesitated in the threshold. Glancing around the small room, she stepped inside and peered under the stall door. "Are we alone?" she whispered.

Crimson peeked under the other stall. "Seems that way."

Laila nodded and waved a hand at the door, chanting a locking spell before turning to Crimson. "I'm not supposed to tell anyone this, but under the circumstances, I think it's only fair if you know."

"I'm listening."

"When a high priestess is sworn in, another high-ranking witch calls on the goddess for a prophecy. I was that witch."

Crimson straightened. The prophecy of a high priestess was held as the utmost of secrets, so Laila had her full attention.

"It was a lot of cryptic, convoluted language like most prophecies are, but one line stands out, and I think you should know." She hesitated, confliction dancing in her eyes. "The line said, 'Red will take you under.'"

Crimson blinked, stunned. "Red will... Seriously? That could mean so many things."

"All I did was channel the message. It's obvious how she's interpreting it." Laila lifted her hands. "Please don't let the others know I told you. I don't want to be next on Rosemary's chopping block."

"Of course. I'll take it to the grave."

"If you can actually beat Rosemary, the entire coven will thank you. And Crimson…" She touched her arm. "You've got the power. If only you could get past your block." She waved a hand in front of the door, removing her spell, and left Crimson alone in the restroom.

With a sigh, Crimson repeated the incantation to lock the door and tried the knob. It didn't move. "That spell worked at least."

Maybe if she practiced, she could pull this off. With her dad's help, the angels could grant her a miracle. Hell, maybe she could convince them the situation was dire enough for them to fix her magic so she could channel the goddess and puke those rainbows for Sophie. But would the coven accept her as their new high priestess? Could she even handle the job?

She waved her hand in front of the door to release the spell, but it wouldn't budge. She tugged on the knob, jiggling it and chanting a reversal incantation, but the lock held tight.

"Oh, for crying out loud." She jerked the knob, twisting it with all her might, and the damned thing came off in her hand. Still the door stayed sealed. "Well, that's friggin' fantastic."

She'd asked, and the universe had answered.

The spell would wear off eventually, but spending the rest of the night locked in a bathroom wasn't the least bit appealing. Setting the broken knob on the paper towel holder, she put one foot on the edge of the sink and hoisted herself up to the narrow window near the ceiling. Her heel slipped off the porcelain, leaving her dangling from the sill as she cursed her misfiring magic for the eighty-seventh time tonight.

All those yoga classes came in handy, and she managed to scramble up the wall and shimmy through the window before tumbling into the courtyard behind the bar. Her hip smacked the ground, but she caught herself with her hands before she could faceplant on the pavement.

"Goddess help me. Can anything else go wrong today?" She clambered to her feet and dusted off her pants. "Never mind. Please don't answer that."

She brushed her hair from her face, retrieved her dignity from the cobblestone, and strutted back inside the club.

CHAPTER FOUR

Mike leaned an elbow on the bar and sipped his whiskey, trying not to look too creepy as he watched Crimson interacting with her friends, which, since he was a demon, was a difficult task. Her curly black hair flowed just past her shoulders, and that clingy blue sweater dipped low on her chest, giving him a glimpse of dark brown flesh that made his mouth water for more. Heat flashed in his eyes, which meant they were glowing red, but he couldn't help himself. That woman lit a fire beneath every masculine urge in his body, making him boil over with desire.

"Hey, Mike." Asher nudged him with an elbow. "Your demon is showing."

Tightening his grip on his glass, Mike squeezed his eyes shut and forced himself to turn around. "Happens every time I see her."

"Why don't you do something about it?"

"Believe me, I've tried. She's like a glass of water in the seventh level of hell. Impossible to obtain."

"You thinking of sending her to Satan, then?"

"Oh, hell no. You'll freeze ice on the Devil's ass before I'll let that bastard get ahold of her. I want to date her, not damn her." He'd come to The Tipsy Leprechaun to check out the witches, but no one here reeked of enough wickedness for him to make a deal with a clear conscience. He was about to call the night a waste—until Crimson walked through the door.

With those sexy high heels on, she stood about six feet even, which put her lips at the perfect height for kissing. It had been nearly a year since he met her, and he hadn't forgotten about the New Year's kiss he missed out on.

Asher pulled his phone from his pocket and groaned. "Satan's balls. I thought I was finally going to get some time off. I cleared my roster, and the bastard added five more names to it."

Mike glanced at the list on the screen. "At least the souls you take to the underworld are already dead. I'm sick of doing the Devil's dirty work."

Asher returned his phone to his pocket. "You get a month off in between."

"And you get to do your job guilt-free." Asher was a reaper. A descendent of Charon, he wasn't a demon, but he could travel in and out of hell at will. His sole job was to track down the spirits of the dead and escort them to whatever part of the underworld their behavior in life afforded them.

"You got me there, but man, I could use a vacation. I'd go somewhere quiet. Maybe a secluded beach in the Caribbean. It'd be nice to sit in the sand and watch the waves with a woman under my arm. If I could find a woman comfortable enough with death to date a reaper." He blinked and shook his head. "Damn you and your advocate magic. I'm not looking for a deal."

Mike chuckled. "I'm not offering one." Sure his palm tingled a bit, itching to seal a contract, but Satan was after a witch. A reaper had nothing to offer the Devil than what he was already required to give him.

"Have fun with your witch. I've got work to do." Asher gulped the rest of his beer and strode out of the club.

Have fun with his witch. Oh, Mike could think of all kinds of ways to have fun with a woman like her, if she'd give him the time of day. *Shit.* Raking a hand through his hair, he pushed from the bar and flagged down the waitress. He could sell swamp water to a Cajun. He could at least convince Crimson to give him a dance.

He ordered another round of drinks and sauntered toward the table where Crimson and Sophie sat. "Your glasses are empty, ladies. Allow me to remedy that for you." He set the wine in front of Sophie and offered the vodka sour to Crimson.

She hesitated to take it. "I don't accept drinks from strangers."

He grinned. "Good thing I'm not a stranger then."

"Oh, come on. It's Mike." Sophie swatted Crimson on the arm. "He's one of Trace's best friends." She took a giant gulp of her wine.

Crimson reached for the drink, and he pulled it away. "It's because I'm a demon, isn't it?" He hoped that was it and that he hadn't misread the heat in her gaze every time she looked at him.

"I…" She bit her lip.

"That's what I thought." He sucked down half the drink and set the glass on the table, cringing at the sweet and sour combination. No doubt she'd heard hellish stories about demons growing up. His defensiveness kicked in despite his best efforts to subdue it. "I'm half human, so I can't be all bad."

"Sometimes humans are worse."

Sophie nudged her again and gave her a look that said they'd already had a discussion about him. That was a good sign. Perhaps Crimson's desires from New Year's Eve were flaring to life again.

He suppressed a smile. "You make an excellent point, but you're generalizing. I take offense to that." He was about to launch into a negotiation, which was his specialty, after all, to convince her to give him a chance, but she shot to her feet, smirked at Sophie, and took his hand.

"Do you want to dance?" She tugged him to the center of the floor. "I need a distraction so my subconscious can work on my issues, and you seem like the perfect man to erase my worries for a while."

He blinked, missing a beat. He hadn't even laid on the charm yet, but she'd made an offer he couldn't refuse. Mike may have been in hot water with the Devil, but the Fates were smiling down on him tonight. "Nothing would make me happier."

"Can demons be happy?" She placed her hands on his shoulders as the band played "It Had to be You," and they swayed softly from side to side.

With his hands on her hips, he gazed into her dark brown eyes. "You don't know much about demons, do you?"

"Just what I've been told."

"Which is?"

Her gaze dipped to his lips for a moment before returning to his eyes. "That you're trouble and I should stay away."

"Hmm. That's sound advice." He narrowed his eyes, leaning back slightly to get a better look at her. "Who gave it to you?"

"My father. He's an Earth-bound angel."

He grimaced. "Ouch." No wonder she kept her distance. "I don't sense any angel in you, though."

"I was adopted when I was seven."

"I see. Well, as good-intentioned as I'm sure your father's advice was, I'm afraid he's misrepresented us. Some of us. Me, to be exact." Heat flashed in his eyes, and he inched a little closer, sliding his hands to the small of her back. She didn't pull away.

"What does it mean when your eyes glow red like that? Should I be afraid?" She linked her fingers behind his neck.

"That depends."

"On?"

"Demons have stronger emotions than humans. Well, stronger within the range of emotions the particular demon is capable of experiencing."

"And what exactly is your range?"

"I'm half human. I experience them all. My eyes glow when I have strong feelings: anger, fear—though not much besides the Devil himself scares a demon—anticipation, happiness, *desire*."

Her tongue slipped out to moisten her lips, and that little flash of pink sent the heat from his eyes down below his belt.

"Should I be scared of what you're feeling now?"

"Not unless you're afraid of being worshipped like a goddess, licked from head to toe, and experiencing so much pleasure you scream my name until you're breathless."

She laughed. "Wow. You cut right to the chase."

"This is the longest conversation I've had with you since the night we met. I don't want to waste any time."

"Good call. I could walk away at any moment."

"But you don't want to."

She searched his eyes, the look in hers dancing between desire and confliction. She wanted him, of that he was sure. But her preconceived notions about demons were keeping her from regarding him as an individual. From seeing him as a man.

He couldn't blame her. Most demons were downright dreadful. Very few ever developed the higher-level emotions that enabled them to experience things like empathy or guilt, which was why the HA meetings only had eight attendees. But Mike—being half human—was born with a full range of emotions intact. Aside from his abilities to light fire with his hands, get people to confess their deepest desires, and make deals on behalf of Satan, he'd always felt more human than demon.

Leave it to him to be attracted to a witch who was raised by an angel. Getting a date with Crimson might be the greatest challenge of his life, and Mike was always up for a challenge.

"What do you want, Crimson?" He pushed his magic toward her, urging her to open up.

"I want to climb you like a tree and find out if you're really as good as you claim to be." With a quick inhale, she unlinked her fingers and moved her hands to rest on his shoulders again.

"I can make that happen."

"I'm sure you could." She glanced at Sophie, who was busy chatting with a woman at the table next to her. "You don't smell as strongly of sulfur as other demons. If I couldn't see the magic in your aura, I might not even know what you are."

"A side-effect of being half human. I'm sure you could cast a spell to neutralize the scent completely if it bothers you."

"Oh, you wouldn't want me to do that. My spell-casting has me in shit so deep I'm drowning."

"Do you want to talk about it?"

She laughed. "Sure, let me unload my problems on a demon. That'll help." She chewed her bottom lip and stared at his chest, refusing to meet his gaze.

"Give me a chance. You might be surprised." He was tempted to push his magic on her again, but his desire for this woman made him want her to open up willingly this time.

"Unless you have wish-granting powers, I doubt it." She finally looked at him. "What kind of magic do you have, anyway?"

He shook his head. "Recovering demons never reveal their magic."

"Devious and mysterious. I find that oddly attractive."

"I was about to argue that I'm not devious at all, but if it works for you, I'll keep my mouth shut."

"It's working." She slid her hands behind his shoulders, moving toward him until their bodies touched. "I wasn't kidding about what I said earlier…about finding out if you're as good as you claim to be."

Holy hell, the feel of her soft curves pressed against him was enough to bring the Devil to his knees. He held her tighter, angling his face toward her hair and basking in the warm, spicy scent of her magic, like nutmeg and white pepper. He couldn't wait to show her just how good a demon could be.

She inhaled quickly and pulled back, her gaze following a group of witches as they exited the bar. Her jaw ticked, and her posture stiffened before she looked at him and forced a smile.

"Friends of yours?" he asked.

"I thought they were." She rolled her eyes, shaking her head. "That's not fair. Yes, they're my friends. I'm in some trouble with the coven, and no one can or will help me." She clamped her mouth shut.

"Why can't they help you?"

"I screwed up some spells. Big ones…royally screwed them up to the point that someone else had to fix them. The high priestess hates me because… Well, that doesn't matter, but I invoked the Supremacy Challenge. If I don't win the challenge, I'll lose my magic. I came here with Sophie to relax, but… I'm desperate. I should be studying."

Heat built in his eyes again, but it wasn't desire activating his demon magic this time. The burning in his right palm meant his inner demon had found a target. Desperate people were easy to convince.

"Maybe I can help you." His mouth formed the words against his will, and he ground his teeth. *Not Crimson. Anyone but her.*

"Do you have mind control powers? Maybe you can hypnotize the priestess so she can't remember how to work magic. Or wipe her memory completely. That would be nice."

"What do you really want?" He bit his tongue, cursing his demon side. Where was that angel food cake when he needed it? Maybe he could convince Destiny to make it pill form so he could carry it in his pocket.

"What do I want?" Her eyes glazed over for a moment

before she blinked. "To win the challenge. To fix my broken magic, dethrone Rosemary, and make the coven a warm, welcoming place again."

Such a simple desire. So pure it wrapped around his heart and squeezed. "Most people would wish death on their enemies."

"Oh, I'd never wish anyone death. If I had to wish something mean on her, I'd ask you to give her taste buds in her asshole. Let her experience the sensation of eating shit every day. That might slow her roll."

He laughed. "That is diabolical. I like it."

"Can you do it?"

"My magic doesn't work that way." But Satan's sure as hell did. The Devil could give her anything she wanted, so long as she paid the price.

"Well, it was worth a shot. I've still got a month to figure something out."

His spine tingled, his connection to hell sparking like a live wire. She was a witch—exactly what Satan was looking for. He pressed his lips together, but his demon side wanted to make this deal so badly he could taste the bile on his tongue. His jaw worked, the muscles involuntarily trying to pry his teeth apart.

Crimson stepped back. "Are you okay?"

He shook his head and tried to move away, but she grabbed his arm.

"Mike?" Concern filled her gaze.

"What are you willing to trade to get what you want?" The words tasted like day-old coffee grinds on his tongue. Bitter and gritty. "Tell me, and I can help you."

She tilted her head. "That's a good question. Maybe I'm going about this the wrong way. I need to do some more research."

He had to get away. If this conversation went any further, he'd be making a deal for Satan before Crimson realized what he was doing. Digging his phone from his pocket, he grimaced at the blank screen. "Oh, shit. That's my manager. There's an emergency at the restaurant. I have to go."

Her brow furrowed. "I hope everything's okay."

"Yeah. It was good seeing you." He spun around and marched out the door.

Damn that was close. Satan's order for a witch had the demon in him on high alert, but the man had to stay in control. He'd find a witch wicked enough to deserve the Devil's company, and it wasn't going to be Crimson.

He marched his ass straight home and opened the fridge, then dove into his secret stash of angel food cake to subdue his demon.

"Did you scare him off?" Sophie looked at Crimson quizzically as she sank into her chair.

"I don't know what happened." Crimson picked up what was left of the drink Mike bought her and took a sip. "We were talking and getting along fine. I'd decided to take your advice and let him distract me from my problems, but then he freaked. He said his manager from the restaurant texted with an emergency, but I saw his phone when he looked at it. The screen was blank."

"That's weird."

"I know. He'd just mentioned he thought he could help me with the challenge, and then he clammed up and ran away."

"He said he could help you?" Sophie's brows disappeared into her bangs. "Do you think he's some sort of a djinn? I hear those guys are dangerous. You think you're getting your wish granted, but it's never worth the cost."

"Nah. Djinns aren't demons, but it does make me wonder what kind of power he has. He wouldn't tell me." She'd be better off getting the help of an angel, no doubt, but if her dad couldn't get that miracle for her…

"I hear demons never tell. Did you talk about anything else that could have scared him off?"

Heat spread across her cheeks. "He said he wanted to lick me from head to toe, and I told him I wanted to climb him like a tree."

Wine dribbled down Sophie's chin as she laughed. "Maybe you're more woman than he can handle." She held up a finger. "Or…I bet the Devil didn't just let him go. Maybe he had to trade his dick for his freedom."

"Unless he stuffed a zucchini in his pants, I don't think that's it." That was quite a package pressed into her hip when they were dancing close. She shrugged. "Whatever. It's probably for the better. My dad's wings would molt if he found out I was getting it on with a demon, and then I'd never get the miracle I'm about to ask him for."

CHAPTER FIVE

Crimson filled a paper cup with espresso and steamed milk and smiled as she handed it to the customer. "Thanks for visiting Evangeline's. See you next time."

The moment the woman stepped out the door, Crimson turned the key, locking it, and flipped the Open sign over so it read Closed. She'd planned to call her dad first thing this morning, but Tiffany called in sick, which left Crimson alone in the coffee shop all morning. She barely had a moment to breathe all day, and now it was closing time.

She rushed through her cleaning routine, took off her apron, and darted upstairs to her studio apartment. The moment she entered the loft, her nerves settled like they always did when she was near her paints and canvases. Dozens upon dozens of portraits, landscapes, and stylized views of New Orleans' famous landmarks stood on easels and leaned against the walls. It was time for another side-walk art sale to make room for her to work.

Stopping in front of her latest creation, she chewed her bottom lip and stared at the image of the sexy demon.

With his wavy, dark hair combed to the side, he wore a deep red suit and a wicked smile. A wall of fire reached up from behind him, licking at the top edge of the canvas, and he held his hand out as if offering it to shake.

She couldn't blame it on the alcohol—she'd only had two and a half drinks last night—but something had possessed her to paint a portrait of Mike the moment she'd gotten home. Sleep had eluded her until she finished it, and he'd been on her mind ever since.

With a shake of her head, she picked up the phone and dialed her father's cell. "Hey, Dad. How's it going?"

"Crimson, sweetheart, how are you?"

"I'm good. How's mom? Is her collarbone all healed?"

He chuckled. "Between you and me, I think she's better than she pretends to be. She's enjoying the extra attention."

"I can't say I blame her." She dropped onto the sofa and leaned her head back. "Listen, I was wondering if you could do me a favor."

"Anything for my favorite daughter."

"I'm your only daughter. Does that also make me your least favorite?"

"Let's hear the favor, and I'll let you know."

She explained her situation with the coven. Her dad was all too aware of her misfiring magic—it was why he'd been assigned to take care of her when her birth mother died. With a witch and an angel as her adoptive parents, her goddess-channeling magic should have been honed to a razor-sharp edge. Instead, it was jagged and crumbling like an eroding riverbank.

"Anyway, it's going to take a miracle for me to win the challenge, so I was hoping you could maybe put in a good word for me with the miracle department?"

He sighed. "Crimi, sweetheart, you know I'd do anything in the world for you, but angels can't get involved with Earthly magic."

Her heart thudded against her chest. Not him too. "I know that's not true. My magic was the reason you adopted me."

"I adopted you to protect you. Your mom did her best to continue your training, but when your birth mother unlocked everything at once the way she did… You were too young for goddess-channeling, and something glitched, but it's not an issue for the angels to solve."

"Well, that glitch has gotten me into trouble. I'm going to lose my magic."

"If your life were on the line, then I could get involved. You can survive and even thrive without magic."

"Dad…"

"I suggest you pray to your goddess for help. I'm sure she wouldn't have granted the challenge if she didn't think you could win."

She tightened her grip on the phone. "Or maybe she's angry because I don't channel her magic like I'm supposed to, and this is her way of getting even." *I'm about as useful as a vampire who faints at the sight of blood.*

"You channel her spirit in your paintings. Maybe try connecting with her that way."

"Don't you think I've tried? I painted all night, but she didn't provide me with an answer. When it comes to my magic and the goddess, there's a block that no one, not even the most powerful healer I could find, can unlock."

"Perhaps the answer is there, and you just can't see it."

Unless the answer was a romp in the sack with a sexy-as-sin demon, that was highly unlikely. "I've tried everything. I've hired every necromancer in New Orleans, and not one of them was able to call my mother back from across the bridge to finish unlocking my magic. I don't know what else to do."

"Study. Try your best. I wish I could help you, but my hands are tied in matters of magic. I'm sorry."

She sighed and rose from the couch. "It's okay. It was worth a shot."

"Remember that confidence is key. You're perfect the way you are because what you lack in magical ability, you more than make up for in kindness, generosity, and a dozen other more important traits."

"Thanks, dad. Tell mom 'hi' for me." She hung up the phone and shoved it into her pocket. *Confidence is key, my ass.* His fake it 'til you make advice may have gotten her through adolescence and secured her spot in the coven, but now she was about to fake her way right out of witchcraft.

She plopped onto the couch again and held her head in her hands. Very few memories of her birth mom remained, but the one thing she remembered most was her mother telling her how powerful she'd grow up to be. Crimson wasn't a mere channeler. She was supposed to have the ability to channel the goddess herself. She should have been able to perform any type of witchcraft imaginable, cast any spell with ease.

Minor spells she could usually pull off. With a few successful incantations under her belt, her confidence would grow, and she'd cast harder spells. But it never failed, the moment she thought she'd broken the hex on her powers, she'd screw something up and be back to square one. Confidence level: zero.

When her adoptive mother ran the coffee shop downstairs, she offered healing potions and simple spells to other supes and humans in the know. Crimson could cast those spells without fail when she was channeling her mother's magic. The moment her parents retired and moved to Florida, the spells she'd been casting for years started getting mixed up. Things would shrink when they were supposed to grow. Love spells would affect the wrong people. They failed more than they helped until eventually Evangeline's Spells and Coffee became nothing more than a mundane café.

What if her dad was right? What if the answer was right in front of her, and she just couldn't see it? Dragging her hands down her face, she stared at the portrait of the seductive demon. She'd been ready to bring the man home with her last night, until he freaked out and bolted. He had mentioned he might be able to help her, and she felt the urge to paint his portrait so strongly last night, she couldn't have stopped if she'd tried.

Was she channeling the goddess in this creation? Was Mike the answer? She'd exhausted all her other options, so what did she have to lose?

She stopped by Casa del Burrito, her favorite Tex-Mex restaurant, for a couple of bean burritos while she waited until his restaurant closed, and then she marched her happy butt up the front steps of Honoré's. Yanking on the doorknob, she found it locked—*duh…the restaurant isn't open*—so she rapped her knuckles on the glass in the door.

"We're closed." Mike's deep, sultry voice drifted through the wood, making her shiver.

She leaned toward the jamb and caught a glimpse of him through the window. "Unless you're on the menu, I'm not here to eat." *Real smooth, Crim.* If he ran off last night because she'd turned on too much heat, that was not the best way to gain entrance. "I was hoping we could talk."

His eyes flashed red as he opened the door. "What if I *am* on the menu?"

"Then I'll have a feast." She fisted her hands. "God, why do I always blurt out this shit when I'm near you?"

He chuckled. "God has nothing to do with it."

"Obviously." She stepped into the restaurant, and he closed the door behind her.

"What did you want to talk about? Are you here to take me up on my offer of worship?" He grinned wickedly and slipped behind the bar to take a white pastry box from a mini fridge. When he bent over, she got a nice view of his backside, and as he grinned over his shoulder, her cheeks burned. "Like what you see?"

She should not have been this attracted to a demon, but everything about him—his muscular body, strong jaw, devilish eyes, and cocky personality—drew her in, making her want to say to hell with all her problems and just lose herself in his arms.

But she wasn't here to get down and dirty with a demon, no matter how hot a flame he lit in her core. "Let's get one thing straight: sex is not on the table."

"You're right. The bed would be more comfortable. I've got a rocking recliner upstairs that might be fun as well." He wiggled his brows and set the box on the bar.

She opened her mouth to speak, but an image of him naked in said recliner, her straddling his lap, flashed behind her eyes, and the words got stuck in her throat.

He nodded. "The recliner it is."

"No." She shook her head, trying to shake away the image. "We're not having sex."

"Well, that's no fun."

"You're a demon, Mike. I know you talk like this to all the women. It's your nature."

He opened the box and paused, his eyes narrowing. "I'm afraid you don't know anything about me if that's what you think of my nature."

"So you don't ignite a fire in every woman you touch, bringing all their carnal desires to the surface?" Because that's what he did to her every goddamn time he looked at her.

Picking up a white pastry, he placed a piece in his mouth, chewing slowly and swallowing before answering, "People do like to tell me things, yes. The Devil deals in desire, but…" He took another bite of cake and leaned toward her, resting his elbows on the counter.

"I don't create desire; it comes from within. So if what you're feeling is carnal, and I do hope it is, that is entirely your own emotion. I just get the luxury of hearing about it. If I'm lucky, maybe you'll show me too."

"You are full of yourself, aren't you?"

He shrugged. "You've told me what you want. I can't help it if it's me. Would you like some angel food cake? It's divine."

"A demon eating angel food cake. That's rich."

"It's light and fluffy, actually." He offered her a piece, but she shook her head, so he returned the box to the fridge. "If you didn't come to tell me how badly you want me to make you come, why are you here?"

"Last night, when I told you about the Supremacy Challenge, you said you might be able to help me. What did you mean? Do you have some kind of power that can fix my magic? What can you do?"

"Ah." He strode around the bar to stand in front of her. "I simply meant to be chivalrous. I'm always game to help a damsel in distress."

She stiffened, and the hairs on the back of her neck

stood on end. "I don't need chivalry, and don't you dare call me that ever again. I may be in distress, but I'm a strong, confident woman, not a damsel." She should have known the goddess wouldn't guide her to a demon for help. What the hell was she thinking coming here? "I should go."

"Stay, please." He gently placed a hand on her arm. "I didn't mean to offend. How can I make it up to you? Aside from help with your challenge, what do you want?"

"I want to know you." The words tumbled from her lips before she could stop them. That was his magic talking. He somehow reached inside people and made them reveal their innermost desires, but there had to be more to it than that. "I want you to tell me about your magic. This getting people to tell you everything they want, does it have a purpose?"

"A recovering demon never reveals his magic."

"Not even to people you're close to?"

He tilted his head. "A few close friends know, but you'll never get it out of them. A lot of trust must be built before I can discuss it."

"So…" She opened her arms. "Let's build some trust."

"I'm intrigued." He ran his gaze down her body and back up to her eyes. "How do you suggest we do that?"

Her stomach bubbled, but she couldn't tell if it was in reaction to his heated gaze or the bean burritos she devoured on the way over. "By talking, and neither one of us runs out on the other if we say more than we mean to."

"It's a deal. Would you like to come upstairs for a drink? I promise to keep my hands to myself until you tell me otherwise."

Oh, lord. What was she doing? Upstairs, into his home, was the last place she needed to go. The man was trouble with a capital T, but she couldn't help herself. She did desire to know him. Maybe his magic wasn't the thing that would help her with the challenge, but she had been compelled to paint him. Any time she felt compelled to create art, it was always the goddess talking to her. Who was she to ignore a deity?

"Do you have whiskey?" She needed something stiff—other than his dick—if she was going to see this through.

"I certainly do." He took the pastry box from the fridge and motioned toward a staircase in the back.

"Whiskey and cake? Is that a good combo?" She followed him to the steps.

"I'm afraid I can't live without it."

Mike shoved another mini angel food cake into his mouth on the way up the stairs, and the tingling in his palm subsided. He gestured to the couch for Crimson to sit and placed the nearly empty box on an end table. Hopefully he'd ingested enough angel magic to keep his demon side at bay, but he'd polish off the rest if need be. Satan could rot in his own circle of hell. This witch would be Mike's.

Crimson sank onto a cushion and ran her hand over the plush chocolate fabric. "For some reason I expected your house to be decorated in red."

He offered her a whiskey and sat next to her. "That's the Devil's signature color, not mine. I prefer earthier tones."

"I see that." She sipped the drink and glanced around the room. The blank screen of the television mounted to the wall cast a distorted reflection of them on the couch, and a potted succulent sat on a table near the window. "Everything looks so normal."

"Were you expecting fire and brimstone?"

"I suppose I was."

He tossed a spark toward the fireplace, setting the log ablaze. "Better?"

"Impressive." Heat flashed in her eyes as her gaze landed on the beige rocking recliner adjacent to the sofa, and she sipped her drink, glancing at him as if expecting him to make a racy comment.

He'd made a promise, though. She said sex was off the table, so he'd be a good boy…until she wanted him to be bad.

The painting on the wall behind him caught her gaze, and she gasped. "That's mine."

"Technically, I bought it, so it's mine."

"You bought one of my paintings?" Her eyes widened in awe.

He nodded. "At a sidewalk sale in front of your coffee shop. You're an amazing artist, by the way." He turned to take in the work of art, a rendering of the Mississippi River done in rich hues of green, gold, and blue. "Your work is divine."

"Well, I can't take all the credit. I channel the goddess when I paint. She speaks through me, expressing the beauty of nature and her love of New Orleans."

"Wow. *That's* impressive."

She shrugged as if it were no big deal. "Channeling is my inborn power. I'm supposed to be able to channel the goddess to cast spells too, but something went wrong when my mother unbound my magic. A glitch, so to speak, because of how young I was." She took another sip of her drink. "So the only goddess channeling I can do is through my painting."

He looked at the beautiful piece of art and then at the gorgeous woman sitting next to him, and his chest tightened. "That makes me love my purchase even more. What was the last thing you painted?"

"Oh, I'm sure it was another landscape or something." She finished off the drink and set the glass on the coffee table. "What about you? Tell me something about Mike the demon. How did you come to live in New Orleans?"

"I bought this restaurant and moved into the apartment above." He set his glass next to hers, scooting closer until their knees bumped.

She glanced at the spot where they now touched. "And the Devil just let you go? Seems like Earth would be crawling with demons if it were that easy."

"I won my freedom in a poker game." He rested his arm on the back of the sofa.

"Seriously?"

"Five Card Draw. I called his bluff and won the game. Satan loves to gamble."

"I bet."

He chuckled. "The Devil did, and he lost. Now I get to live topside as long as..." Gazing into her dark eyes, he brushed a strand of hair from her forehead.

"As long as what?" She drifted closer to him, and the warm, spicy scent of her magic tickled his senses.

"As long as I keep my powers in check." He almost slipped and told her about the monthly payments he made in exchange for his freedom. Something about her made him want to open up and share everything about himself. Maybe this was what people felt like when they talked to him. The difference was, she wasn't using any type of hocus pocus to make him feel this way.

"When a demon wins his freedom, he keeps his magic? It seems like the Devil would strip you of your powers when he set you free."

"Satan prefers us to keep our demonic tendencies. He likes us to struggle. Being a recovering demon isn't easy."

"Which is why you go to AA meetings?"

"*H*A. We're hellions, not alcoholics. Well, most of us aren't alcoholics."

"We're friends now, right?" This time, she didn't just drift toward him. She lifted her butt off the couch and scooted until her hip pressed against his.

"I sure hope so." Holy Hades, the woman smelled heavenly, and the heat radiating from her skin sent all the blood from his head straight to his groin.

"Then you can tell me what other kind of magic you have." Her breath against his ear sent a shiver down his spine.

"That's a tricky subject, I'm afraid." He turned his face toward hers.

"How so?" She leaned toward him, her nose a scant two inches from his, and paused.

He nearly went cross-eyed trying to meet her gaze as he fought the urge to take her mouth with his. Damn him for making such an ill-conceived promise to keep his hands to himself. He had no willpower around her. "When you're a demon, people automatically judge you if they know your magic. I'm half human, yet no one can see past the demon side. I'd like you to get to know me before you judge me."

She rested a hand on his thigh. "I'd like to get to know you too."

Oh, damn it all to hell. He promised to keep his *hands* to himself, but he didn't say anything about his lips. He moved closer, tilting his head and gently brushing his lips to hers. When her breath hitched, he couldn't help himself, and he took her mouth with his.

Her lips were soft as velvet, and as she tightened her grip on his thigh, a shudder ran through his body. She tasted like whiskey, his favorite flavor, and her kiss was so hot, a ground fissure could have opened up with a blast of hellfire beneath him because he was about to go up in flames.

"Are you sure you don't have this effect on all women?" she whispered against his lips.

"The self-preservation instinct keeps most women away." He kissed her jaw before gliding his lips down to her neck.

She laughed. "I guess that's another part of me that's not working right, then." Cupping his cheek in her hand, she pulled his mouth to hers and kissed him again.

Devil have mercy, this woman was alluring. He slid a hand behind her neck, pulling her closer, the man in him completely in control. The angel cake had done its job subduing his demon. In fact, the urge to make a deal with this witch completely vanished from his mind.

A deep rumble sounded from her stomach, and she pulled away, clutching her abdomen. "Uh oh."

"Are you okay?"

Her eyes tightened, her gaze cutting between him and the exit. "I think…" Her stomach whined and groaned as if she'd swallowed a hell cat. "Can I use your restroom?"

"Sure. It's through the bedroom to the left." He pointed toward the door, and she shot to her feet, darting through and slamming it behind her.

Holy charro beans, that was a close one. Crimson barely made it to the bathroom before her protesting dinner reached its grand finale, and damn, did it end with a bang. And speaking of beans, what the hell did Casa del Burrito put in those things? Jet fuel? Hellfire? That shit burned. Literally.

She had tried to ignore the churning in her gut as she made out with Mike. His lips were soft and his body firm, and while her brain had attempted to tell her it was wrong to want a demon, every other fiber of her being had screamed at her to go for it. It had been hard to tell if the heat building in her lower abdomen was from desire or dinner, until it hit critical mass and she had to make a run for it. And not a moment too soon.

The second her butt hit the seat, the bomb dropped. She turned on the water and faked a few coughs to cover up the sound, and thank the goddess the plumbing worked properly. But now, she stood at the sink in a cloud of funk that smelled worse than a Bourbon Street dumpster on Mardi Gras.

What the hell was she thinking eating Tex-Mex before going to see a hot guy?

She rummaged through the cabinet beneath the sink, but all she found were a few spare rolls of toilet paper. Leave it to a man to not keep a bottle of Poo-pourri, or any type of air freshener, on hand.

The linen closet only contained linens, and in the medicine cabinet sat a single jar of face cream. Demons needed to moisturize?

She opened the jar and sniffed. Unscented, of course. Not that she could have used a cream to neutralize the stench she'd created. What would she do? Smear it on the walls?

Think, Crim. Think. She could cast a spell. A simple incantation to freshen a room. Her mom used to do one every morning in the coffee shop to enhance the aroma of the brew. People loved the smell of coffee. Now, how did that spell go?

She ran the verse through her mind a few times to make certain she'd get it right. Then she straightened her spine—confidence was key—and recited the words: "Aroma rich, scent pure. Enhance the fragrance, increase it sure."

Her stomach burned—with magic rather than digesting food this time—and as the warmth spread, rolling down her arms, she cast it into the air.

Oh, shit.

That spell didn't cover up odor, it magnified it. Damn it, she knew that. She *knew* the spell intensified the scent of coffee, so why did she think it would have the opposite effect on this problem?

Because being near Mike short-circuited her brain. That's why.

She shook her hands and paced the small space. Pine. The scent of pine or fir...any conifer...would help to cover this up. She took a deep breath, immediately regretting that action, and spoke another incantation. "Fragrant pine, cypress, fir, enhance this space with conifer."

The smell of Christmas trees filled the room, but it did nothing to mask the other odor tainting the air. *Crap.* Now it smelled like someone ripped a massive fart in the woods.

Mike tapped on the door. "Are you okay in there?"

"Fine." Aside from the fact she was choking on the

stench. If she opened the door now, the smell would knock him over. It was probably seeping through the cracks already. *Oh, please, Mother Earth, open the ground and swallow me whole.* "Be out in a minute," she said in her most cheerful voice.

"Take your time."

As his footsteps receded, she yanked aside the shower curtain, desperately searching for something…anything to squelch the stench.

A window!

Thank the goddess. Stepping into the tub, she worked the pane open and fanned the air outward. But the night was stagnant, and with the door closed, no cross breeze encouraged the air in the bathroom to escape.

She peered through the window, down to the grassy courtyard below. It wouldn't be *that* far of a fall if she hung onto the ledge and lowered herself all the way before letting go.

Two bathroom window escapes in as many nights didn't say much for her dignity, but what choice did she have? She couldn't open the door and face Mike when his entire apartment would soon reek of Casa del Burrito discharge. She could never face him again.

This was what she got for trying to interpret a message from the goddess that wasn't there. She'd come here for her own selfish reasons, and this was her punishment.

So much for getting it on with the hottest demon in town. He was probably a beast in the sheets too.

The toxic fumes stung her eyes as she cast one last glance at the door, grabbed her purse, and climbed out the window. Luckily she'd worn flat shoes, so she didn't twist an ankle on the fall, but the impact jarred her joints, and she bit her tongue.

She swallowed the coppery taste from her mouth and trudged through the side yard to the street, leaving her dignity in the dirt where it belonged this time. It wouldn't be *that* hard to avoid Mike for the rest of her life, especially if she lost the challenge and had to move away. Even sadder…she needed to find a new favorite Tex-Mex restaurant.

CHAPTER SIX

Crimson leaned on the counter in the empty coffee shop, scouring the encyclopedia of magic her mom had overnighted to her four days ago. Ever since her walk of shame from Mike's house, she'd spent every spare second she had studying and practicing the myriad spells she could be called upon to cast for the challenge.

Avoiding him the past few days had been easy since she'd barely left the building, but she couldn't stop berating herself for screwing up a possible relationship before it even began. Despite her angelic upbringing, she was really starting to like him.

She couldn't get the man off her mind, and it was messing with her nightly painting ritual. Every time she picked up a brush and opened herself to channel the goddess' divinity, the only thing her hand would allow her to paint was portrait after portrait of the sexy demon. She'd memorized every cut and dip of his chiseled features, and she couldn't help but remember the way his lips felt pressed to hers as the brush glided across the canvas.

Focus, Crim. She'd blown it with Mike, and there was no coming back from that level of mortification.

A bell chimed, signaling the entrance of a customer, and she spoke with her gaze trained on the spell she was trying to memorize. "Welcome to Evangeline's. What can I get for you?"

"What are you offering?" The deep, velvety voice wrapped around her like a piece of silk sliding over her skin.

Her jaw clenched shut, and she lifted her gaze to find the object of both her desire and humiliation standing across the counter. Her throat thickened, her tongue feeling like it had turned into a giant cotton ball. Attempting speech was completely pointless, so she grabbed a menu and handed it to him.

He set it aside and slid onto a stool, folding his arms on the counter. "You disappeared the other night. I didn't know witches had teleportation powers."

Heat spread from the bridge of her nose across her cheeks, all the way to the tips of her ears. "We don't. I… uh…went out the window."

He nodded. "That's why it was open. I thought it was because of the smell."

Oh, sweet goddess, please send a wolf to devour me now. She knew she needed to speak, but what in the name of the triple goddess could she say? Clutching the countertop, she cast her gaze to the white marble.

"What happened in there?" he asked.

The heat from her face spread to her chest, and a bead of sweat dripped down the back of her neck. She slammed the encyclopedia shut and gripped the spine. "Were you going to order something?"

"Talk to me, Crimson." He put his hand on top of

hers and caught her gaze. "Let's *clear the air*." His lips twitched like he was trying really hard to suppress a smile.

The sentiment must have been contagious, because laughter bubbled from her chest before she could stop it.

"There she is." He squeezed her hand and let it go.

"Oh, god." She clutched the book to her chest. "I'm so sorry." Squeezing her eyes shut, she shook her head. "I had Tex-Mex before I came over that night, and it didn't agree with me."

He chuckled. "That's an understatement."

"That wasn't." She sighed. "The smell was… I was embarrassed, so I tried to cast a spell to diminish the odor. Instead, I intensified it."

"And the pine scent?"

"After I magnified it, I tried to cover it up. I have a bad habit of screwing up spells, and I was mortified. We were just getting going, and then I stunk up the entire building. I should have just…well, I don't know what I should have done, but escaping through the window wasn't it." She rubbed her temple, cursing herself for making a bad situation worse. Did she honestly think she could avoid this man for the rest of her life? "I'm an idiot."

He drummed his fingers on the counter. "I'll tell you what. Let's start over. Have dinner with me tonight. I promise we'll go somewhere light on the stomach." He winked.

She looked into his eyes, and though they were filled with amusement, they also held sincerity. Second chances in life were few and far between, yet this demon was offering her just that. "Can we pretend the other night never happened?"

"We'll never speak of it again."

Her ears cooled, and though she'd never recover

completely from the mortification, if he was willing to forget it happened, she'd give it a try. "Deal. Pick me up at seven?"

His eyes flashed red, and he squeezed his hands into fists before dropping them into his lap. "Seven works for me. What are you reading?"

She turned the book around to show him the cover. "I'm studying for the challenge. We each have to cast a series of spells, but we won't know which ones until the challenge begins. Not only do I have to cast them correctly, but I have to do it better and faster than Rosemary."

"You mentioned a glitch in your magic. Aren't you going to try to fix it first?"

"If there were a way to fix it, I would have found it by now. Believe me, I've tried everything. So, I'm going to win this the old-fashioned way. By hard work and determination."

"That's the honorable way to do it."

She set the book down and sighed. "Honorable, yes, but it's not likely to work. Honestly, I'm not even sure I want to be high priestess. I only challenged Rosemary because I panicked. I tend to act without thinking sometimes."

"No windows for you to climb out of?" He grinned.

She laughed. "Not at the time, no. She was about to bind my powers and make me human, so I spouted off the challenge. Now, if I lose, I'll become human *and* be exiled, never to speak to another witch again."

"That's harsh."

"I know. I should have just let her bind my powers. Now I'm going to lose everything: my home, my friends, this coffee shop that's been in my mom's family for generations."

She opened the book and sliced her finger on a page. The wound stung, and a drop of blood pooled on her skin. "Damn it. Papercut." She stuck her finger in her mouth to quell the bleeding.

"Do you need a bandage?"

She shook her head. "It's fine."

"Well, I think you'll make a fabulous high priestess when you win the challenge."

She let out a sardonic laugh. "Thanks. I sure don't want to lose everything. I swear though, sometimes I think I'd sell my soul to Satan if he could make this all go away. Can people really do that?"

Mike grimaced and set his fisted right hand on the counter. "Don't say things like that. You don't mean it."

"Does the Devil really make deals like that?"

"All the time."

She shook her head. "Hell, if he can make it so this challenge never has to happen, and things can go back to the way they were, he can have my body too."

His eyes flashed red, and he uncurled his fist, holding his hand toward her. "Satan accepts your offer."

"It's a deal." She laughed and placed her hand in his. "You're from hell. It can't be *that* bad a place."

His palm heated, and her papercut sizzled before the wound closed completely. She tugged her hand away and examined her finger. "You have healing powers?"

The color drained from Mike's face. "You were joking, right? You didn't really want to sell your soul to the Devil, did you?"

She waved a hand dismissively. "Of course not. My dad would molt if I did something that stupid."

"Good." He nodded and rose to his feet. "You really shouldn't joke like that, especially around a demon."

"Point taken. I'll be more careful with my words." She tilted her head. He was still pale. "Are you okay?" Had she screwed things up again by joking about selling her soul? That would be her luck. Or maybe healing her papercut had drained him.

"Yeah." He rubbed his palm on his jeans. "I've got some things to take care of, so I'm gonna go."

"Hey." She stepped around the counter and rested a hand on his bicep. Thankfully, he didn't pull away. "I'm sorry for kidding around about Satan. I haven't spent much time with demons, and I didn't mean to offend you."

He leaned toward her and pressed his lips to her cheek. "We're good."

His breath on her skin made her shiver. "See you at seven?"

"I'll be here." He stroked the backs of his fingers down her cheek before stepping out the door.

Holy hell. What the ever-loving fuck have I done? Mike stalked down the sidewalk and ducked into a secluded alley before waving his hand and opening a portal to his home. He landed in his living room and dropped onto the couch, raking his fingers through his hair and pulling it at the roots.

He made a deal. *Damn it!* He'd stuffed his face with half of a full-sized angel food cake before he went to see Crimson. He shouldn't have been capable of striking a bargain like that. With that much angel magic flowing through his system, he shouldn't have been able to send Satan a testicle, much less a body and soul.

It didn't happen. She was joking, so it couldn't be legit. He'd subdued his demon side with angel magic. Hell, he'd done everything but hog-tie the beast, and Crimson didn't mean it. But if it wasn't legit, then why the fuck did his spine tingle and his palm burn like hellfire when they shook? And that sizzle? That was blood. Sure, it was from a papercut and not a purposeful wound, but the Devil didn't care about details like that. She'd said the words, and Mike had accepted on Satan's behalf.

I'm a fucking idiot. He deserved to spend eternity in the tarpits for this. *Hell's bells and buckets of blood!* He had to fix this.

Taking the back staircase to avoid the restaurant, he marched his ass over to Sweet Destiny's and threw open the door. The soft floral scent of angelic magic folded around him, making his demon side squirm, but he forced himself across the threshold and rang the bell on the counter. A melodic *ding* filled the air, and his neighbor drifted from the kitchen into the storefront.

Her copper hair flowed down to her shoulders, and her fair skin held an ethereal glow. Peach lips curved into a comforting smile, and her voice reminded him of a cool stream running through a meadow. "Is it Thursday already? Let me box up your order."

"No, it's not. I need your help."

Her smile brightened. "I'm happy to assist. Tell me what you need."

"Those cakes, the most recent batch, they had the usual dose of magic?"

"Of course. Just enough to subdue a demon without causing harm. Is there a problem?"

"And the full-sized one you made for me? It's the same?"

"Yes…"

"So if I ate half the full-sized cake…"

Her eyes widened. "I'd say you're lucky you're half human. That much angel magic in one sitting would render a full-blooded demon catatonic for hours."

"So it should have squelched my magic, right? I shouldn't have been able to seal a deal after eating that much cake."

Her brows scrunched. "Well, I don't know. Did it *feel* like the deal sealed?"

"Maybe. Fuck. Yeah, it did, but she didn't mean it. She was joking when she said it. Well, maybe only half-joking, but I know she didn't mean it. She's good. Pure. She doesn't belong in hell."

Destiny pressed her palms together and closed her eyes for a moment. When she opened them, they held sadness and compassion. "I'm afraid I can't help you. The only person who knows if the contract is good is Satan himself. You'll have to ask him."

"Satan…" he growled.

Destiny raised her hands. "Please don't call him here."

Mike nodded and stormed out the door. He focused on the tingle in his spine, activating his direct line to Satan —if the Devil could use it for emergencies, so could he— but the tingle turned to a buzz…a metaphysical busy signal.

"Figures." He stomped through the back door and darted up the stairs, glancing at the clock on the way in. Four p.m. He had exactly three hours to take a trip to hell, tell Satan he could shove that deal where the sun doesn't shine, shower, and pick Crimson up for their date at seven.

Plenty of time.

With a wave of his arm, he opened a portal to hell, but he hesitated to step through. He'd been topside for five years straight and had sworn to never set foot in the bowels of the underworld again. While his demon side exulted in the heat seeping through the opening, his human half wanted to puke.

But he'd be damned for all eternity before he'd let his sweet Crimson become a pawn in Satan's chess game of life and death.

Swallowing the bitter bile from his throat, he stepped through the portal, his heart missing a beat or twelve as the gate slammed shut behind him.

The demonic entrance to hell looked just as he remembered, with stone floors worn smooth from millennia of footsteps crossing over them and jagged, cavernous walls towering high above, looming in oppression. The screams of tortured souls echoed off the walls, and Mike froze, listening to the horrid sounds.

His lips tugged into a smile as he recognized the skip at the end of the loop before the cacophony started up again. Those screams weren't real. They were from the "Pits of Hell" soundtrack that came from a topside Halloween store back in the nineties. Satan piped it in through all the gates to get the demons riled up and to scare the shit out of the new souls entering the realm of the dead.

Mike flipped up the collar on his jacket and kept his head down as he made his way over the rocky terrain toward Satan's palace on the hill in the distance. This was to be a quick in and out mission. He didn't have time for run-ins with family and old "friends." His mother had disowned him when she'd heard the news of his plans to move topside, but not before she tried to chew his ear off —literally—over the ordeal. The other advocates never cared for his half-human nature, and now, with his demon subdued, he couldn't afford a challenge from one of his old associates.

A moat of molten lava surrounded the Devil's obsidian castle, but even that was just for show. Demons were impervious to heat and flame, and the witch's magic used to seal off this section of hell from the dead was impenetrable.

He crossed the bridge and pressed his palm to the hot plate on the exterior wall. A human's skin would melt off the bone if they touched metal this hot, but Mike's demon side rendered him immune to heat like a full demon.

A loud *thunk* echoed from inside as the lock disengaged and the door swung open. Red glass spires soared six stories up to the rocky ceiling, and blood-colored velvet drapes hung from the windows, blocking the view of the cave surrounding the palace.

Making a sharp right, he paced down the expansive hallway toward the Devil's office and halted in front of the door. He lifted his fist and froze, unable to make his knuckles meet wood.

Don't be pathetic. His mother's words echoed in his mind. *You don't belong up there. You'll continue to damn the innocent, whether you want to or not.*

"Not this time, Mother Dearest." He pounded his fist against the door.

Heels clicking on the stone floor echoed from inside, and a moment later, the door swung open.

"Hello, I'm Esmerelda." A witch with short black hair, styled into a pixie cut, greeted him. Tall and slender, she wore a silk shirt and pencil skirt in the standard red Satan required of all his office employees. "How can I help you?"

He stepped into the waiting room, stopping in front of a red velvet couch. A massive fireplace took up the entire wall across from it, and flames licked all the way to the ceiling. This must be what Crimson imagined Mike's apartment would look like.

"I need to see Satan. It's an emergency."

Esmerelda shook her head. "I'm afraid that's not possible. He's on vacation."

Mike opened his mouth to respond, but as her words sank in, he paused. "Vacation? The Devil never takes a vacation."

She shrugged. "He does now. Would you like to leave a message for him?"

Satan, the Lord of the Underworld, had taken a vacation and left this witch in charge of his office? Hope filled his chest like a hot air balloon. Did this mean…? "Are you his new assistant?"

"Oh, no." She waved a hand dismissively. "I'm just filling in until his advocate finds a permanent replacement. I made my deal directly with the Devil before I died, and being his hand servant wasn't part of it."

"Damn."

"We all are." She laughed. "His new girlfriend thinks he works too hard, so she insisted he take her on a trip. They're on a transatlantic cruise and won't be back for three weeks."

Three weeks stuck in a tiny cabin on a cruise ship? "That sounds like pure hell."

"I'm sure it is. There's a rather foul drug lord on the same cruise. It's my understanding that Satan plans to spread a nasty stomach virus among his crew."

"Sounds diabolical."

"The man can't get away from work, can he?"

"Speaking of work, do you have access to his deal manifest? I need to check it for a name. There was a mix-up, and I'm not sure the last deal I made for him went through."

"Oh, you're an advocate? I should have known with your good looks." She strutted toward the assistant's desk and sank into a swiveling chair. "I'm afraid everything's been frozen and locked in his absence. New souls are being stored at the docks, and deals are hanging in limbo until he returns. You'll have to come by when he gets back."

"Thank you. I appreciate your help."

She smiled. "Anytime."

His hands curled into fists as he marched out of the palace and made his way to the demonic exit. Satan would be gone for three weeks, which meant Crimson's soul was safe for the time being, and Mike had twenty-one days to find an actual wicked witch who could take her place.

He tore open a portal and stepped back into his home before plopping in front of the computer and pulling up The Haunt Ads website. The Haunt Ads was like Craigslist, but for supes only. With a few clicks of the trackpad, he took out an advertisement.

Wanted: Personal Assistant to the Prince of the Underworld.
Requirements: Must be a witch with a heinous nature.
Willing to spend eternity in hell.

He deleted the *eternity in hell* part and changed it to *Willing to live in the underworld in Satan's palace.* That sounded much more appealing.

If the ad didn't work, his only other choice would be

to coerce someone, but he hadn't used trickery to make a deal in decades. Could he even pull it off? He'd have to quit the angel food cake and avoid Destiny and the other angels at all costs. All the work he'd done to subdue his demon would have to be reversed. He'd become diabolical again. He'd have to if he wanted to save Crimson from his stupid mistake.

He swallowed the thickness from his throat. Would she even want him if he went back to his demonic ways? The woman was raised by an angel, after all. But he'd rather her hate him for the rest of her life topside than hate him from the hell he'd damned her to.

He rose to his feet, stripping out of his clothes on the way to the shower. Even he could smell the sulfur on his body after spending twenty minutes in hell. With the hot water blasting from the faucet, he scrubbed until his skin went raw.

The ad had to work. He'd find the Devil a new assistant, and he'd win the heart of the beautiful witch while he was at it.

CHAPTER SEVEN

"That was a fantastic play." Crimson slipped her hand into Mike's outside the Saenger Theater on the corner of Canal and Rampart, at the edge of the French Quarter. A streetcar rumbled by as they walked hand in hand, and they turned on the sidewalk, heading deeper into the Quarter.

"I'm glad you enjoyed it. The Greek's version of hell was actually the most accurate of all religions." Mike had taken her to see *Hadestown*, a musical account of Orpheus traveling to the underworld to save his fiancée, Eurydice, and while he could appreciate the story, sitting that close to Crimson, their knees touching, her hand resting in his, had been the highlight of his evening so far.

"Really? That's fascinating." She placed her free hand on his bicep.

Before the show, they had dinner at a small café on Rampart, where Crimson ordered a chicken salad sandwich with a side of fruit. She'd given him a pointed look both when she placed her order and when the food arrived, as if waiting for him to make a comment about the bathroom incident. Much like the Devil himself, however, an advocate always kept his word.

Now, as they shuffled down the sidewalk away from the crowd, the cool night air caressing his skin, his phone pinged with an incoming message. The first inquiry into his ad for the Devil's assistant made his heart jump into a little sprint. He shoved the device back in his pocket, the weight of his accidental deal with Crimson lightening. He could fix this. He *would* fix this. Tonight, he would simply enjoy her company.

"Such a sad ending, though. He should have trusted her." She faced him as they paused on the corner of Dauphine Street, her dark eyes glinting in the lamplight. She wore a deep emerald-green dress that showed off her curvy figure and mulberry lipstick he couldn't wait to be covered in. "They made it so far, but I bet she probably wouldn't have been allowed to leave whether Orpheus looked back or not."

"Satan enjoys the struggle, but he never goes back on a deal. A promise is a promise."

She inched closer, resting her hand on the lapel of his charcoal jacket. "But this was Hades, not Satan."

He placed his hand over hers. "He's had lots of names over the years, but he's always been the same guy."

"Really? Did you know him back then?"

"Nah. I'm not *that* old." They crossed the street. "I was going to ask if you wanted to grab a coffee, but seeing as how you're around it all day, I'm going to guess that's a no."

"Actually, I'd love to." She grinned, casting her gaze downward. "I know a place that serves the best latte in town. They're closed, but I think I can convince the owner to let us in."

She'd been acting shy since he picked her up this evening, and he could only imagine she was still embarrassed. This was the first sign they might be able to get back on track, and he wasn't about to waste the chance. Gliding his fingers along her jaw, he gently lifted her chin. "Are you asking if I want to go back to your place?"

"If I was, what would your answer be?"

He took her hand, lacing his fingers through hers. "It would be an adamant 'hell yes.'"

"Good, because that's exactly what I'm asking."

When they turned the corner, a couple stood in the middle of the sidewalk, blocking their path. The man glared at the woman, the hurt in his eyes battling with disbelief as he shook his head.

"So that's it?" the man asked. "You're going to pack your bags and move to Nashville with some dude you've known for a week?"

"We should go around." Crimson tugged Mike's hand, but he stopped, pulling her to his side.

"Hold on. I want to see how this plays out." The woman's true desire might as well have been painted on her face in bright red ink, but the guy was absolutely clueless.

The woman crossed her arms and shook her head, tossing her long blonde hair behind her shoulders. "He asked me to, so why not? It's not like there's a reason for me to stay here."

The hurt in the man's eyes was palpable, but it seemed the woman was just as blind as he was. "Well, if that's how you really feel, then go. Have a nice life."

"We really shouldn't be watching them fight," Crimson whispered.

"Seriously, Austin? You're supposed to be my best

friend. The least you can do is be supportive of my decision."

Austin scoffed. "I'm not going to support you ruining your life over a man you hardly know, Anna. I hope he's worth it."

Austin turned to go, and Anna caught his hand. "Wait."

"Why?" He pulled from her grasp. "What do you want from me?"

"I want…" Tears collected on Anna's lower lids.

Mike rolled his eyes. Humans could be so dense sometimes. How could two people, who were supposedly best friends, be completely blind to each other's feelings? It wasn't like love was a difficult emotion to grasp.

He rested a hand on the woman's shoulder. "Tell him what you really want, Anna. What's your true desire?"

Her eyes widened as she looked at Mike, and when she turned her attention to Austin, her bottom lip trembled. "I want you to tell me to stay."

Austin's posture softened. "What? I thought you wanted to go to Nashville."

Anna shook her head as Mike gave her an extra push of magic to overcome the stubbornness. Finally, she spoke the truth, "I want you to love me like I love you." She dropped her arms to her sides and slumped, exhausted from the weight of carrying the secret for so long.

"Your turn, Austin." Mike clapped him on the shoulder. "Tell her what *you* want."

"All I've ever wanted is to be with you. I've been in love with you since eleventh grade."

Anna gasped. "Why didn't you ever say anything?"

"Because you made it clear you wanted me to stay in the friend zone."

"I don't want you in the friend zone. I love you, Austin." They hugged, and Crimson gaped as Mike tugged her away.

"That was…wow!" She bit her bottom lip and looked at him with wonder in her eyes. "I did not see that coming."

"I couldn't help myself. Humans act so stupid when it comes to their emotions, especially where relationships are concerned." He wrapped an arm around her shoulders. "If you want someone, you should tell them. It's simple."

"Is that so?" She slid her arm around his back. "What if you've done something so embarrassing, you're surprised you're even able to face the person you want?"

"Hmm…" He feigned deep thought. "That could throw a wrench into the situation. Good thing nothing like that has ever happened to us, right?" He winked, and she laughed.

"Are you sure you don't have any angel in you? That was a very good deed you did back there. It's something my dad would have done."

He stopped walking and faced her. "Hasn't anyone ever told you not to compare a demon to an angel? Say that to the wrong person, and hellfire will shoot out his horns, setting his hair ablaze."

She paused, her mouth opening and closing a few times as she processed his words. "I'm sorry. Please don't catch fire."

He laughed. "I'm joking. Demons aren't flammable."

She narrowed her eyes, gazing at the top of his head.

"I don't have horns either. See?" He tilted his head down and ran his hand through his hair. "You weren't kidding when you said you didn't know much about demons."

"You're the first one I've gotten to know."

"Let me guess. You thought I was watching that couple argue because I enjoyed the conflict."

She flinched and shook her head. "No. I wasn't thinking that at all. I didn't know why you stopped. Maybe you were looking out for her safety because the guy looked pissed."

He chuckled. Demons were masterful liars, but it seemed witches were not. At least, this witch wasn't. But she was still here, by his side, strolling through the French Quarter with a demon, despite her angelic upbringing. He must have been doing something right. "Austin wasn't pissed; he was hurt. The woman he loves was about to leave him for a stranger."

"How did you know that? I thought you got people to *tell* you their deepest desires. With that couple, you already knew."

"You could see it on their faces." He pressed his lips together and continued walking. Even if he hadn't possibly damned Crimson to an eternity of servitude in the underworld, it still would have been too soon to share his magic with her. She was raised by a man whose mission was to save souls, and Mike's job for the past eighty years had been the exact opposite.

"Maybe *you* could see it." She shook her head. "It's usually men who are the clueless ones about emotions. You are full of surprises, aren't you?"

"I've got a few up my sleeve for when I get you alone, if that's what you mean." His eyes heated at the thought of all the devilish things he had planned for her, and he ran his hand down her back to give her butt a squeeze.

She laughed. "Now the demon is coming out. I'm not sure which side of you I like better."

"Lucky for you, I'm a package deal." He moved his hand to her hip, tugging her closer to his side. "You get both."

"Ooh, a man on the streets, a demon in the sheets? I can't wait."

"Neither can I."

Wow. Crimson couldn't wipe the stupid grin off her face as she walked, wrapped in Mike's arms, toward her home. Everything her dad had told her about demons was a lie. Well, not a lie—angels weren't capable of fibbing—but a gross over-generalization about a complex and diverse species of supe.

Mike was kind, sincere—*good,* even. Was it right to call a demon good? After the way he'd helped that couple get over their fears and admit their feelings for each other, she couldn't call him anything but.

"What are you grinning about?" He brushed his fingers down her cheek, sending a shiver up her spine. "You have a gorgeous smile, by the way. What's it for?"

He did say if a person wanted someone, they should say so. What did she have to lose? "It's for you, Mike. I like you."

"Of course you do. What's not to like?" He winked, and heat bloomed low in her belly.

Cocky. There was another word she could call him. He was drop-dead gorgeous; he had a way with people, and he knew it. But he wasn't annoying about it, so maybe cocky wasn't the best word. Confident? *Confidence is key.*

Whatever it was, it lit a fire inside her, and she wanted to strip him bare and make him beg for mercy. The thought of a man like Mike trembling beneath her touch had her hotter than a love potion boiling in a cauldron on high heat. Forget coffee. She planned to head straight up to her apartment, and this sexy demon would be the main course.

They turned the corner onto Royal and found a woman leaning over a storm drain, wailing into the hole in the concrete. "Chopper! Come, Chopper. Come!" She reached an arm into the drain and pulled it back sobbing.

After the marathon of horror movies Crimson watched last week, she half-expected the woman to pull out a bloody stump, but thankfully, her arm remained intact. She rushed toward her and knelt by her side. "Are you okay?"

The woman sniffled. "It's Chopper. He fell down the drain."

Crimson peered into the darkness—though she didn't see anything—as Mike stopped next to her. "What's Chopper?" he asked.

"He's my dog."

"Your dog?" Crimson squinted and looked into the small rectangular hole. The name Chopper conjured images of a pit bull or German shepherd, but unless Chopper was a shifter, there was no way a dog that big would fit down the storm drain.

"He's a chihuahua, and he's my baby," the woman sobbed.

Mike patted her shoulder. "We'll get him out."

She nodded and looked into his eyes. "Can you also find a man to love me? I'm so lonely, and Chopper is all I've got. I haven't had a date in six months, and I just want someone to love me."

She clutched Mike's bicep, and he pried her off. *Poor*

guy. "One thing at a time. How long has he been down there?"

"About ten minutes." She wrapped her arms around herself.

Crimson shined her phone's flashlight into the hole, and it reflected off a tiny pair of eyes just out of arm's reach. "He's here. I see him." But there was no way in hell they could grab him.

Mike got on his hands and knees next to her and peered into the drain. "There are rats bigger than Chopper down there."

She suppressed a chuckle. "People unload their problems on you a lot, don't they?"

"Yep. It's all part of the magnificent package."

A package she couldn't wait to unwrap. But she couldn't leave with this poor little pooch trapped in the gutter. "So far, all your magic seems good. Got any that can save a rat-sized dog from the sewer monster?"

He looked at her. "Nothing I can do in public. Can you cast a levitation spell? Something to lift the little guy enough that we can grab him?"

Now, there was a thought. She'd just practiced an incantation to move objects yesterday, and it had worked...for the most part. She might have shattered a salt shaker the first time she tried, but the third time was the charm for that spell.

Then again, this was a living animal. What if she shattered Chopper?

"I don't know if that's a good idea."

Mike sat back on his heels, lowering his voice. "I could open a portal and travel through, then hand him to you from below. But, I'm not sure Chopper's momma could handle seeing that. If you levitate the dog, she won't be able to detect the magic from where she's standing."

Crimson shook her head. "I'm a bad witch. I screw up most of my spells."

"What happened to hard work and determination? Crimson, I know your greatest desire is to not be 'broken,' and I promise that you're not. You only *feel* broken."

"Mike…" She *was* broken. Always had been, always would be.

"Name one spell you've screwed up since the night we danced at the bar."

She snorted. "How about the one in your bathroom?"

"Did you screw up the incantation, or did you simply cast the *wrong* spell?"

"I…" She clamped her mouth shut. When her mom used that spell, it was meant to intensify the aroma of the coffee shop. And when Crimson used it, the spell worked exactly right, *intensifying* her problem. Come to think of it, she'd managed to pull off all of the minor spells she'd been working on since she started training.

He rested a hand on her back. "You can do it. I have faith in you."

She nodded. Confidence was key, and if Mike thought she could do it…

"Please!" the distraught woman moaned.

"All right." Lying on her stomach, Crimson reached both arms into the drain and whispered the spell she'd practiced yesterday. Chopper whined and backed away, not allowing the magic to take hold.

"C'mon, little guy. Hold still for me." She whispered the spell again, willing the goddess' magic to flow through her, focusing all her power on the dog, and he squealed as she magically lifted him into the air. Her hands closed around the tiny, trembling body, and she passed the pooch to Mike before clambering to her feet and dusting off her knees.

She did it! She used her magic, and it didn't backfire. Sure, it was a simple spell, but it was important for the situation. Excitement bubbled in her chest. Maybe she could pull off this challenge after all.

"Oh, my sweet little puppykins. Mommy is so sorry you fell down the holey-woley. Are you okay?" The woman kissed the dog, and Chopper licked her in return, bathing her entire face in doggy slobber.

Man, she really does need to find a date.

With the woman and her dog reunited, Crimson took Mike's hand and led him toward her building. "Wow. Two good deeds in one night. Aren't you going to burst into flames now?"

"Nah, demons are impervious to flame, remember?"

"I'm sure Satan doesn't like it though. Does he give y'all hell when you do good deeds?" They paused in front of the entrance, and she took her keys from her purse.

"As long as I make my monthly payments on time, he leaves me alone." He clamped his mouth shut and swallowed hard as if he'd said more than he intended.

"Monthly payments? Is it like mafia protection or something?"

He glanced at the ground. "Something like that."

"That doesn't surprise me at all." She wanted to ask exactly how much he had to pay for his freedom each month, but she refrained. He'd open up when he was ready, and right now, she was ready to make him scream her name.

Bypassing the coffee shop entrance, she opened the

door leading to the stairwell and dropped the keys back into her purse. "I'm on the third floor."

He lifted a brow. "No coffee, then?"

"Do you *want* coffee?"

"Not really." He grinned, moving toward her. "Do you?"

She rested her hands on his chest as her heart kicked into a sprint. "I think you know what I want."

He placed a hand on her hip. "Why don't you tell me?"

"I'd rather show you." Gripping the lapel of his jacket, she pulled him across the threshold and crushed her mouth to his.

A moan rumbled in his chest, and she kicked the door shut before pushing him against it, leaning into him as she tangled her fingers in his hair. He was right: no horns protruded from his scalp. The protrusion in his pants, however, pressed into her stomach like a horn of plenty.

"Showing is good. I like showing." He cupped her ass and held her close, grinding against her as he drank her in.

The nagging little voice in the back of her head whispered this was wrong. Mike was a demon with access to people's innermost desires, and though she didn't know what devilish thing he could do with that knowledge, it could only lead to trouble. That's what demons were about.

But Mike was recovering. He went to HA meetings, and he'd been nothing but kind in her presence. As the pesky voice whispered again, she stomped it like a cockroach. She was done playing it safe.

"I'm sure my dress is filthy from saving the chihuahua," she whispered against his neck before grazing her teeth along his skin.

He shivered, his voice coming out more growl than words. "You should take it off then."

"Let's get out of the stairwell." She pulled from his embrace and immediately missed the warmth radiating from his skin.

"Good idea. With the things I want to do to you, we might scare your neighbors."

She laughed and guided him up the stairs. "Sophie is my only neighbor, and she spends most of her time with Trace. I doubt anything we could do would scare her."

"You don't know what I'm capable of."

A thrill shimmied up her spine at his words. The mystery surrounding him was part of the draw, and she couldn't wait to unravel him.

As they stopped outside her door, he stood behind her, his front pressed to her back, his hands roaming her hips while his lips caressed the bend between her neck and shoulder. Her skin turned to gooseflesh, and she dug in her purse, cursing under her breath when she couldn't find her keys.

"Problem?" His lips moved against her skin.

"I've got too much junk in here. I just had them earlier, but now I can't find my keys."

"Need some incentive?" He slid his hands up her stomach to cup her breasts, teasing her nipples through the fabric of her dress.

They tightened into pebbles, shooting a jolt of electricity straight to her core. "Oh, screw it." Reaching a hand toward the knob, she whispered an unlocking spell and threw open the door.

"Impressive." He followed her into the apartment. "The self-proclaimed bad witch has cast two spells in a row without a hitch. I'm starting to think you've been lying about your magic."

"Being near you seems to have a positive effect on me. Go figure."

"Hm." Something flashed in his eyes, an emotion she couldn't read alongside his signature demon red, before they widened and he turned to survey the room. "Color me mesmerized. Crimson, these are remarkable."

Her name rolled off his tongue like warm honey, and she gave him a moment to take it all in. Dozens upon dozens of her paintings lined the walls, the ones on the floor sitting in rows three or four deep.

"These are all channeling sessions with your goddess?" He walked along the wall, examining the paintings.

"Not all. Some come from my own mind, but they're mixed in." As she watched him admiring her work, her lips tugged into a smile. It felt nice to be around someone who appreciated her talents rather than pitied her inadequacies.

"I can't tell the difference. You're an incredible artist. Simply mesmerizing."

With his attention temporarily captivated, she might as well use the time to duck into the bathroom to make sure her stomach didn't have any surprises in store. "I'm going to freshen up while you recover from your mesmerization."

He caught her gaze, and his eyes smoldered. "Don't be too long."

Her stomach fluttered—in a good way this time—and she stepped into the restroom. Her dress was ruined, with black street-gunk smeared across the front, but her hair and makeup held up, though her lips were swollen from that amazing kiss.

With her confidence in her spell work at an all-time high, she whispered a quick spot-removing incantation. Her dress shimmered, and the street-gunk dissolved. *Damn.* Three in a row. Mike was as good for her magic as he was about to be for her libido.

She returned to the loft and found him studying the portraits she'd done of him. They were hidden behind a stack of landscapes, so he must have flipped through her entire collection to find them. Now, he had all three side by side, leaning against the wall.

The flutter in her stomach turned sour, and heat spread across her cheeks. "That's um… You weren't supposed to see those."

His smile brightened his entire face. "Why not? I'm honored you painted me. Though, this one…" He taped the first painting of him in a red suit, sitting on a throne. "I hope you weren't channeling the goddess on this, because I will never be the ruler of hell."

"I think it's metaphorical." She collected the paintings and laid them on a table, tossing a drop cloth over them. "That was after the night at the bar, when you walked out on me. My mind was racing."

His eyes tightened. "Right. Sorry about that."

"We seem to have a habit of running out on each other."

"Not anymore." He moved toward her, taking her in his arms. "You cleaned your dress. Another spell gone right?"

"Yep. It's a good thing I didn't really sell my soul to the Devil, huh? It seems I don't need his help after all."

His eyes darkened for a moment before he shook his head. "Let's not talk about that."

"Let's not talk at all." Linking her fingers behind his

neck, she jumped and wrapped her legs around his waist. He caught her by the hips, his demon strength holding him steady as she crushed her mouth to his.

With one hand, he tugged down the zipper on the back of her dress and popped open her bra with a twist of his fingers. His palm was hot against her bare skin, and as he brought it up to cup her neck, she let her feet slide to the floor.

Stepping back, she shimmied out of her clothes and stood before him in nothing but a pair of black satin panties and her heels. The red in his eyes turned liquid, his expression that of a predator who'd zoned in on his prey. *Absolutely thrilling.*

"Take off your clothes. Now," she ordered.

He blinked, then a sly grin curved his lips. "Yes, ma'am," he drawled as he shrugged out of his jacket and unbuttoned his shirt. "Would you like me to dance for you too?" He wiggled his hips as he tossed the garment aside and unbuckled his belt.

The man was solid muscle, hard and defined like he was carved from stone, yet she'd felt the tenderness in his touch. The passion in his kiss. She yearned for more.

"You've been holding out on me, Magic Mike. What else can you do?"

With inhuman speed, even faster than a vampire—and she'd had her way with a vamp or two, so she knew what they were capable of—he stripped off his clothes and pinned her to the wall. She gasped as his mouth closed around her nipple, and he gently sucked it, hardening it into a pearl while he roamed his hands over her body.

She returned the gesture, exploring the cuts and dips of his muscular frame. The sulfur on his skin was so faint she could barely smell the tell-tale demon scent, but the fragrance of his human side, warm and woodsy, permeated her senses, making her mouth water. She could never match him in strength, but she was determined to make his knees weak.

He glided his tongue up the side of her neck and nipped at her earlobe. "Is sex on the table tonight, love?"

She wrapped her hand around his dick and stroked him, reveling in the way his lids fluttered with her touch. "The table, the couch, the bed. Where do you want to have it?"

He groaned, the deep rumbling sound sending a shiver down her spine. "Right here against the wall sounds good."

"Does it?" With Mike thoroughly distracted, she grabbed his shoulders and spun him around until he was the one pinned. She grabbed his dick again, and dropping to her knees, she circled her tongue around the head.

"Holy hellhounds." His voice came out as a raspy whisper, and he dropped his head back against the wall.

She took as much of him into her mouth as she could and slowly pulled back before taking him again. He exhaled a hiss, and his hands, which had been splayed against the wall, curled into fists.

She continued sucking him, enjoying the masculine grunts and moans emanating from his throat, until his knees began to give. Taking him in her hand again, she rose to her feet and gazed into his hooded red eyes.

"I need you, Crimson." So much raw emotion laced his words, she wondered if he was talking about sex or something more. He cupped her face in his hands as the red in his irises faded to a soulful, deep brown. "I want to worship you for..."

He blinked, the vulnerability in his expression slipping

away, a devilish grin replacing it. Scooping her into his arms, he nodded toward a doorway. "Is that your bedroom?"

"It is."

"I believe I promised to lick you from head to toe." He carried her to the bed and laid her on the mattress. "Let's get started."

The man made good on his promise. Starting with her neck, he worked his way down her body, licking and nipping, raising goose bumps all over. He removed her panties, kissing down one leg and then up the other, all the while avoiding the one place she wanted him to lick most.

"You're teasing me." Her voice sounded breathless.

"I'm a demon. What did you expect?" His tongue bathed her sensitive nub, and she nearly screamed at the electric sensation shooting out to her limbs.

He chuckled, obviously pleased with her reaction, and then he went to town, licking and sucking until the orgasm coiled in her core and released in an explosion of fireworks to rival the Fourth of July. The man had to have a forked tongue with the oral acrobatics he'd just performed.

Wait… Did he have a forked tongue? He was a demon after all.

He rose to his knees and stroked his cock, his tongue slipping out to lick the moisture from his lips. No fork. He was just *really* good with his mouth. "Demons are incredibly fertile, but we don't spread disease. Well, my kind doesn't."

One corner of his mouth tugged into a crooked grin, and for a moment, the vulnerability she'd glimpsed in his gaze returned. "Are you…?"

"I'm on birth control."

He climbed on top of her, settling his hips between her legs, and held her gaze as he slowly pushed inside her. As he filled her completely, his eyes flashed red briefly before returning to their human brown, and they made love.

She'd expected the wickedness to spill over into sex. For him to be all about the physical pleasure, worshipping her body until they both climaxed in a frenzy. But the way he held her, his slow, deliberate movements, his breath against her skin... Everything about this felt like he was also worshipping her soul.

Her heart swelled with the intimacy, and she clung to his shoulders, another orgasm building in her core as his rhythm increased, his thrusts growing harder until he rose onto his hands and looked into her eyes.

Her entire world exploded with the next thrust of his hips. She cried out, her body shuddering as they came together, never breaking their gaze into each other's eyes. Her reality turned upside down and inside out as he relaxed on top of her, stroking her cheek with the backs of his fingers.

Holy hell. She was falling for a demon.

CHAPTER EIGHT

"Your application says you're a witch." Mike eyed the petite redhead from across the table and sipped his coffee. She wore a dark green tunic over light green leggings, and her eyes sparkled like emeralds.

"Oh, I am," she replied in a thick Irish accent, the wart above her lip bouncing with her words. "My great-great-grandmother was one hundred percent witch."

Mike rubbed his temple to ward off the impending headache and glanced over the application again. He'd conducted seven interviews in the past two weeks here, in the private dining area at the back of his restaurant, and so far, not a single applicant had been an actual witch.

They'd all been devious, vile, even downright evil, but not one of them met Satan's number one requirement. His personal assistant had always been a witch, and the chances of getting the ancient bastard to change his ways were slimmer than Frosty the Snowman surviving in hell.

But Mike wouldn't give up. In between interviews and running his restaurant, he'd also spent the last two weeks getting to know Crimson. Falling in love with her. He'd spent every spare second he had with her, watching her practice her magic, her confidence growing with every spell she cast correctly. And the nights spent between the sheets… She could give a succubus a run for her money.

He'd grown used to having her in his life, and he intended to spend forever with her, whether it was here in New Orleans, with Crimson as the high priestess of the coven, or somewhere else if she didn't win the challenge. It didn't matter where he lived, as long as it was topside with his magnificent witch in his arms every night.

He looked at the leprechaun in front of him, his gaze bouncing between her wart and her monobrow, and she glared back. She was ornery enough to spend eternity by Satan's side, that was for sure. "Tell me about your magic."

She disappeared from the chair and reappeared in the corner behind him. "Teleportation." She disappeared again, and the sound of thick heels on the wood floor echoed through the room before she swatted him on the back of the head. "Invisibility." Her form came back into view as she smiled smugly and plopped into the chair. "And demons don't intimidate me. You're not nearly as scary as everyone said you'd be."

"I'm not like other demons."

"I should hope not. I'm looking for murder, mischief, and mayhem. So, do I get the job?" She crossed her arms and arched a bushy brow.

He suppressed a smile. How he'd love to force this little elf on the Prince of the Underworld. If only Satan would accept her. "Can you cast spells?"

"Who needs spells when you can be invisible?" She disappeared and reappeared in a flash. "I also have a knack for finding gold."

"The Devil has no use for gold."

"But I bet you do…" She grinned, revealing rotting teeth nearly the same color as her shirt. What was it with leprechauns and green?

He sighed. Of course she couldn't cast spells. "Satan requires a witch with spellcasting powers. It was listed in the job description."

"You realize you're asking someone to give up their life to spend eternity serving the Devil, right? Witches can pretty much make anything they want to happen become reality. They solve their own problems, yeh know?"

"I realize that."

"Good luck finding one who'll be willing give up her freedom. Most of 'em are too nice for the Devil, anyway. Nature-loving hippies, the lot of 'em."

He knew that all too well, which was why, three weeks closer to his deadline, he hadn't found anyone worthy of damnation. "I'll be making a decision by the end of the week. Thanks for stopping by."

"The Devil'll be lucky to have me." She rose to her feet, though she wasn't any taller standing, and waddled toward the door as Crimson strutted through.

"Hey there, handsome." Her eyes locked with his, and his chest tightened. She didn't glance down to see the tiny woman moving toward her, and they collided, the leprechaun's head smacking into Crimson's hip with a *thunk.*

"Watch where yer goin', yeh hippie." She rubbed her head and glared up at Crimson.

"I'm so sorry. I didn't see you." Crimson reached toward the leprechaun to console her, but as the elf swatted away the gesture, she held up her hands and looked at Mike. "I didn't mean to interrupt. The hostess told me to come straight back."

He closed his laptop. "You're not interrupting. We're done."

The leprechaun narrowed her eyes at Crimson, raking her gaze up and down her form. "Are yeh a full-blooded witch?"

"Yes. I'm Crimson. Are you a leprechaun?"

"Aye. One-sixteenth witch, but apparently that's not enough for the Devil. His advocate won't even give me a chance." She jerked her thumb toward him, and he forgot to breathe.

His stomach dropped into his boots before ricocheting up to his throat, lodging there and making him choke. He'd been outed by a leprechaun. *The little fuck.* He bit the inside of his cheek, fisting his hands in his lap to keep from strangling the horrid creature.

"Advocate?" Crimson stepped out of the leprechaun's way as the elf waddled out the door. "What's going on?" Wariness tightened her eyes, and she clutched her purse strap on her shoulder, staying near the exit.

With a heavy sigh, he flattened his palms on the table and gathered his thoughts. The truth had to come out sooner or later…though much, much later would have been his preference. *After* he'd completed his final job and could tell his witch, with one hundred percent honesty, that his evil-doing days were over.

Instead, he felt exposed. Naked in front of a crowd with stones clenched in their fists. Would Crimson be the first to throw?

He should have damned the little green elf when he had the chance.

"Why don't you join me?" He gestured to the seat next to him. "Are you hungry? I can order lunch."

"I'm fine." She sank into the chair. "Do you…?" She

pressed her lips together, casting her gaze downward before locking eyes with him. "Do you collect souls for Satan? Are you the Devil's advocate?"

The disgusted look on her face tore him in two, but there was no turning back now. He refused to lie to the woman he loved any longer. "It's not always souls. It's…" He blew out a hard breath. That wouldn't matter to her. "I am."

She leaned back in her chair, away from him, her slow nod of understanding turning into a shake of disbelief. "And that leprechaun was bargaining with you? Were you planning to send her to hell before her time?"

"She wanted to go, but I wasn't going to send her. I swear."

"I had a feeling, but…" Her bottom lip trembled as her mouth opened and closed. "I thought you were recovering. That you weren't working for Satan anymore. You said you won your freedom in a poker game, so why…? Why would you still send people to hell?"

He started to ask her for a minute so he could stuff his face with angel food cake before he explained things to her, but his demon side didn't need subduing. Come to think of it, he hadn't felt the need to ingest angel magic since he accidentally shook her hand more than two weeks ago. That was a bad sign.

"I only won partial freedom in that game." He picked at the edge of the laptop, casting his gaze downward. "I still have to make a deal for him once a month in exchange for staying topside."

Her lips parted on a quick inhale. "That's the payment you mentioned before? You don't pay him with money, you pay in souls?"

He reached for her hand, but she slipped from his

grasp. "Souls or whatever the Devil happens to be collecting at the time. You'd be surprised how many men are willing to give up one of their testicles to get what they want." He smiled, hoping to break the tension, but she shook her head.

"I'm trying to stop. I swear I am. The Devil offered me a deal himself to get my full freedom. I had to do one more job for him, and he was going to let me go."

"'Had'? You said that in past tense. If you already made the deal, what were you doing with the leprechaun? What was the final job?"

Hell help him, he had to tell her. There was no way around the truth this time. "Satan needs a new personal assistant. I was supposed to find him one."

She pursed her lips, nodding. "There has to be more to this story."

"He's always had a witch as his assistant, so that was the deal. I find him a witch to be his servant for eternity, and in exchange, I get my freedom."

"I see."

"But here's the thing." He laid his palms on the table and straightened his spine. "For the past few decades, I've been trying to be good. I've purposely sought out those with wicked souls—people who were going to hell regardless—to make deals with. Since I won my freedom, I haven't damned a single undeserving person." *Until now.*

"My ability to see into people, to get them to tell me their desires…that's the advocate magic. I can get them what they want in exchange for a price. But I can also sense evil. I can spot a pure soul, and I only bargain with tarnished ones."

She clutched her purse in her lap, tensing as if ready to

bolt. "So this witch assistant deal. If it's not part of your normal monthly expenses, couldn't you tell him no?"

"I was late on my payment. Very late. He used that as a bargaining chip and gave me a choice. Find a witch to damn, and I get my freedom. Fail, and he takes me back to hell. I'll never see sunlight again. Or you."

She swallowed hard and whispered, "Who did you damn?"

"I didn't mean to damn anyone yet. I was looking for a wicked witch."

Her voice grew louder. "Who did you damn, Mike?"

He hung his head. "I think I damned you."

Silence answered him. He flicked his gaze up to her face, and she sat frozen, expressionless. He waited, giving her ample time to tell him off, to slap him, to storm out. *Something.* But she didn't move. She just looked at him, giving him no clue what might be going on in her mind.

He didn't dare use his magic to pry into her current desires. She probably wanted to castrate him and wear his balls as earrings like Satan's former fling loved to do.

He waited as the seconds ticked into minutes, but she refused to speak. He'd rather spend an eternity with a crow pecking at his liver than endure another second of the silent treatment. "It happened in your café when you joked about selling your soul."

She crossed her arms. "Obviously."

"I tried to get you to stop. I told you not to talk about it, but you kept going. The call was too strong. I couldn't help myself, and I'm sorry." He lowered his head again, unable to meet her gaze.

"Oh, so it's my fault?" Her voice sounded incredulous.

"No, that's not what I meant."

"It better not be what you meant, mister, because I

had no idea your power was making deals with the Devil. I never would have said something like that if I'd known."

"I'm sorry."

Her jaw ticked as she narrowed her eyes. "And whose fault is it that I didn't know?"

"Mine." He slumped farther in his seat, feeling like a scolded child. "I really didn't mean to. I care about you, Crimson, and I never wanted to hurt you."

"You didn't have to. You could just send me to your master and let him do the hurting." Her words stung, but he deserved every slice from her sharpened tongue. "So, that's it then? I'm damned to be Satan's servant for all eternity because of something I said in jest?"

His shoulders crept toward his ears. "You said it, and words are usually binding."

If she'd been part demon, her eyes would have flamed. "I was *joking*. I thought you understood that." She laughed, disbelieving. "Wait. Back up a minute. You said you *think* you damned me, and words are *usually* binding. Why don't you know for sure?"

"The Devil's on vacation."

"Vacation? I suppose he went down to Georgia? Is he searching for a soul to steal? Oh, wait. He has *you* for that."

Mike sighed. She might as well slice him open and disembowel him. He deserved worse. "He's on a three-week transatlantic cruise. I can't check the manifest until he gets back, so there's still a chance—since I confirmed you didn't mean it right after we shook hands—that it didn't take."

She tapped her foot. "And the leprechaun?"

"I put a listing in the Haunt Ads, and I've been interviewing potential candidates for two weeks. I was hoping to find someone who would take the job willingly, but no pure witches have applied."

"You're as bad as Orpheus."

"Orpheus?"

"He didn't trust Eurydice, and he damned her because of his stupidity. You should have trusted me. I know a lot of witches. I could have helped you."

He opened his mouth to reply, but the words wouldn't come. What could he say? He'd been so concerned about Crimson not liking him if she knew what he really was, he never considered asking her for help. "We keep our magic a secret for a reason. Aside from the other demons, only Trace and Destiny know what I am. I was afraid to tell you."

"Why? Do you think I can't see the goodness in you? Do you think I'm so dumb that I wouldn't be able to look past the job you were born into and see the man you've become?" She shot to her feet and paced in front of the table.

"I'm sorry, Crimson. I'm going to fix this. That leprechaun will make a perfect assistant to the Devil. I just have to convince him to give her a shot."

"And if this deal is sealed…if my joke has damned me, is there anything I can do to stop it from happening? What if I win the trial on my own, without the Devil's help? What if I refuse his assistance?"

He stood and stepped toward her. "Satan's deals are binding."

She continued pacing. "So there's absolutely nothing I can do?"

"I'm afraid not. The Devil never reneges on a deal, and he won't let the other party back out either. All we can do is find a replacement, someone he'll like better."

She whirled to face him. "Maybe that's all *you* can do."

"We can do it together."

"Oh, no. It's too late for that. You've had weeks to tell me what was going on, and the only reason it came out now was because I nearly flattened a leprechaun. I've never cared for potato pancakes, and I don't like your bullshit either." She turned on her heel and marched to the door.

"I'm going to fix this," he called, but she didn't turn around.

"Go to hell," she shouted as the door swung shut behind her.

That was exactly where he needed to go, as soon as the Devil got home.

CHAPTER NINE

What in the goddess' name was Crimson supposed to do now? Roasting in the underworld for all eternity would be pure…well…hell. Not to mention what the heat and humidity would do to her hair.

She stormed into her apartment and slammed the door, the impact vibrating across the wall, sending a framed picture of her parents crashing to the floor. The glass shattered on the wood, but Crimson ignored the mess and made a beeline for her laptop.

Mike's hands may have been tied when it came to undoing a deal with the Devil, but Crimson was raised by an angel, for goddess' sake. Surely the whole gotta-keep-things-in-balance rule would apply here. Aside from lacking the genetics, she was practically an angel herself.

Double-clicking the video chat app, she called her dad and dropped into a chair. Her computer dinged as the call connected, and her father's image filled the screen.

"Good afternoon, sweetheart. How's the spell work going?" Her dad laughed as her mom stepped into view.

With her dark hair swept back into a tight twist, she

wore pink sweats, and her arm was cradled in a dark blue sling. "Did the encyclopedia of magic I sent you help at all?"

"Yes, it's been great. I'm getting better at the spells."

"Oh, that's wonderful news." Her mom sank onto the sofa next to her dad. "I wonder if you can convince the council to reevaluate the challenge? If your magic is getting better, maybe—"

"I've got a bigger problem." She rubbed her forehead, scrambling for a gentle way to tell them what she'd done, but she came up empty. She might as well shoot straight. No matter where she aimed, the arrow would come back to hit her in the ass. "I might have accidentally told a Devil's advocate that I'd give Satan my soul if he'd make this whole challenge mess go away."

She braced herself, expecting the slew of curses to flow from her mom's mouth, the feathers to drop from her father's wings. Instead, they sat quietly, their gazes slowly lowering before they looked at each other.

Tears collected on her mom's lower lids. "It didn't work."

Her father's jaw set, his face becoming a mask of stone. "Fate deemed it so. We did all we could."

"Am I missing something?" Crimson leaned her elbows on the desk. "What are y'all talking about? What did fate deem?"

"Your birth mother…" Her dad's voice was low and rumbly, as close to a growl as an angel could get.

"It's not her fault." Her mom put a hand on her dad's knee. "She was the messenger. Witches channel prophecies, but we don't create them ourselves."

"Did my birth mother receive a prophecy about me?"

And they'd kept it from her all these years? Her mouth hung open as disbelief gnawed at her gut.

"We have to tell her." Her mom gave her dad a pointed look.

"I hoped it wouldn't come to this." Her dad's expression softened, and he looked at her with sadness in his eyes.

Her mom patted his leg and scooted closer to the computer. "When your birth mother found out about the cancer, she called on the goddess for a prophecy. She wanted to prepare you for whatever the future might hold, but what she learned was…" She shook her head.

"What, Mom? What did she learn? Did she know this was going to happen? Was it about my magic? My soul? Tell me!"

"In the first prophecy, she learned you were meant to channel the goddess in your magic and your art. That's why she unbound your powers all at once, so you'd have the best chance of fulfilling your destiny. But the ability to channel the goddess' magic isn't obtained overnight and never at such a young age. That part of your magic couldn't be unbound until you were older." She tilted her head, casting a look of sympathy. "Your mother didn't live long enough to complete the process."

Crimson's heart ached at the memory of her mother, but this wasn't new information. She'd been dealing with misfiring magic her entire life, and she knew it was because her mother didn't unlock everything. "What does that have to do with my current predicament?"

"As her disease progressed," her dad said, "and neither magic nor medicine could cure her, she begged the goddess for another prophecy." He slipped his hand into her mom's. "She wanted to know how things would turn out for you, and…she learned you'd sell your soul to Satan one day."

Crimson blinked, her face going slack with shock. "You *knew* this would happen, and you didn't think it might help to clue me in?"

"We were trying to protect you." Her mom's voice trembled.

"Wait…what did the prophecy actually say? You know those things are cryptic as hell."

"Crimson…" her dad admonished.

"Sorry."

He inhaled deeply, hesitating to tell her. "It said… 'The man from hell will finish her.'"

Her mom nodded. "It's why your father was assigned to adopt you. Your mother begged the archangel to interfere in your destiny. The powers that be thought if you were raised by a witch and an angel, you'd have the best chance of avoiding your fate."

"My fate." A sinking sensation threatened to drag her to the ground, so she clutched the sides of the chair. How could they let her live her entire life without this information? If her fate was predetermined, and they were trying to intervene, why would they keep it from her?

Her head spun, and she squeezed her eyes shut for a moment to still the dizzying sensation. When she opened them, both her parents stared at her with pity in their eyes. "Don't you think it might have been pertinent to share this with me sooner? If I'd known, I never would have…"

She clamped her mouth shut. They didn't need to know how close she'd gotten to Mike. They weren't the only ones who could play the secrets game.

"We tried our best, sweetheart," her dad said. "I

thought if I instilled a fear of demons in you that you'd avoid them. How did this happen anyway?"

"Seriously? If anything, you made me more curious. All my life you taught me to see the good in people. To look past their vices and examine their souls. But not demons. You said even the ones in recovery were evil, but that's not true, is it? Demons can have goodness in their hearts."

He let out a heavy sigh. "Some of them can, yes."

She groaned. "So there's nothing else you can do to help me? Raising me to avoid demons was your best effort, and nothing you can say to your superiors will change their minds?"

"I'm afraid their hands are tied," her dad said.

Her mom nodded. "Fate's a tricky bitch."

Her dad cut a sideways glance at her mom. "When is the challenge?"

"In three days."

"Your mother and I will get on the first flight. We want to be there for you when—"

Crimson held up her hands. "It's not going to happen." Their hands were tied. Mike's hands were tied. Was she the only one left with the will to take on the Devil himself? She might have enjoyed a little bondage in the bedroom, but *no one* would tie her down in life.

Her dad leaned toward the computer. "Crimson, sweetheart, you can't stop fate."

"Watch me. I'll talk to you later." She slammed the computer shut, and as the anger boiled in her chest, she swiped the contents of her desk to the floor.

Pencils scattered across the room, and the laptop hit the wood with a crack, but it didn't matter. Those things would be of no use to her in hell.

A knock sounded on the door, followed by Sophie's muffled voice. "Everything okay in there?"

Crimson stomped to the door and threw it open. "Never better. I'm dating a demon who damned me to hell, and apparently my parents have known it was going to happen since they adopted me."

"What happened?" Sophie strode into the loft and plopped onto the couch. "Sit. Talk."

"I can't sit. I feel like I'm going to explode." She paced the length of the sofa and explained her ordeal. "Who knew joking with a demon would land me a life sentence in the underworld?"

Sophie blinked. "Wow. Okay, first, you need to settle down before you actually do explode. I'm not cleaning glittery witch goo out of the rug."

She dropped into a chair. "I knew dating him was a bad idea."

"Did you? Or is that your dad talking?" She shook her head. "Doesn't matter. Let's focus on the problem at hand. Does Mike know you were joking? If so, that should negate the contract, right?"

"He said it doesn't matter because I said the words aloud. And…" She picked at her nails. "If I'm honest, I have to admit I was only half-joking. At the time, living in hell sounded better than being human."

"Well, that's a problem."

"Tell me about it. I'm so furious at him. If he'd have just told me what was happening, what his magic was, I could have helped him. At the very least, I'd have known to keep my mouth shut instead of making jokes like that."

Sophie nodded, resting her elbow on the arm of the couch. "Sounds like he screwed up."

"Royally." She dropped her head back on the chair. Of

all the men in all of New Orleans, why did she have to fall for the most dangerous one? Oh, right. Because it was her fate.

Sophie leaned her chin in her hand. "He said he didn't mean to make the deal with you, though?"

"He practically blamed me for it when we argued, reminding me he told me not to say things like that." Another spark of anger flared in her chest. *Damn him, and damn fate.*

"Did he tell you not to say it when the deal happened? Did he try to stop you?"

She shrugged. "Yeah."

Sophie nodded thoughtfully. "Did he apologize?"

"He did, but he should have trusted me, dammit."

"He should have. You're right about that." She leaned her elbows on her knees. "But does he have a way to fix it? Is he trying?"

"He mentioned a couple of ideas, but I really thought my connection to the angels would help. I stormed out before he could explain everything."

"Wow. Sucks to be him. Good thing we don't make mistakes, huh? It must be awful to screw up your magic, try to make it right, and then have the person you affected not forgive you." She leaned back on the sofa and pretended to pick lint from her pink blouse. "I can't imagine what that would feel like. Can you?"

Crimson narrowed her eyes. "Do you have a point?" But she already knew the answer. Jax still hadn't forgiven her for turning him into a cat, and that bothered her more than she cared to admit.

Sophie held up her hands. "I'm just saying this sounds like a classic pot and kettle scenario. Or maybe it's a glass house. Either way, you care about him, and he's your only chance at getting out of this with your soul intact."

Crimson closed her eyes for a long blink, letting her friend's words sink in. Sophie was right. She did care about Mike. She may have gone into the relationship simply looking for a distraction, but he'd grown on her. He'd proven demons could escape their nature and be good. If he could break from his destiny, why couldn't she?

She grabbed her phone and dialed Mike, but he didn't pick up. Swiping open the message app, she typed *Please call me* and sent the text. "I'm an idiot."

Sophie stood. "No, you're a badass witch who's going to make fate her bitch."

"You're right." Crimson rose to her feet and strode to the door. "But first, I have to find Mike."

CHAPTER TEN

"Damn Haunt Ads," Mike muttered to himself as he shuffled up the path to Sweet Destiny's. They'd pulled his ad from their site and canceled his account, citing a violation of their terms of service.

Apparently, Satan had struck a deal with the owners a few years back guaranteeing them a profitable business in exchange for not letting demons utilize their services in relation to their jobs. *Fucking Devil.*

He paused in front of the bakery, a two-story, nineteenth-century house painted pristine white with sky blue shutters that belonged on a cloud floating in heaven. Destiny kept the place immaculate, taking *cleanliness is next to Godliness* to a whole new level.

As he opened the waist-high wrought iron gate to enter the front porch of the angel's business, his demon side recoiled. His stomach clenched, and heat rolled through his body in response to the divine magic, but he forced himself inside.

After nearly overdosing on angel food cake when he first started dating Crimson, he'd laid off the magical delicacies lately in hopes that his demon side would be able to strike a deal for a new satanic assistant. But with the interviews complete and the ad no longer running, he'd run out of potential candidates.

He still held on to the sliver of hope that the deal didn't take, but it would be another few days before Satan returned to hell and opened the registry to find out.

Stepping into the seating area of the bakery, he found his reaper friend, Asher, sitting at a small pink table, scowling and stuffing a massive piece of cake into his mouth. Asher gestured to the chair across from him, and Mike forced a smile, sinking into it. He had two hours before he had to be at the Hellions Anonymous meeting, so he could spare a minute for his distressed friend.

"You okay, man?" Mike asked.

Asher closed his eyes, letting out a slow breath as he chewed and swallowed the chocolate cake. "Who'd have known the best devil's food cake would come from an angel's bakery?"

A bit of brown frosting marred his chin, and Mike wiggled a finger at his face. "You've got a little…"

"I was saving it for later." Asher swiped a napkin across his face and dropped it on the table. "Chocolate makes everything better."

If only. "Eating your emotions? I'd think with the Devil on vacation, you'd have a lighter workload."

"You didn't hear? That banshee he was dating nearly drove him insane. He left the cruise before the stomach virus hit its peak, and he's back in the underworld, ornerier than hell."

Mike's heart missed a beat or two before slamming against his chest. "He's back?"

"Yeah. And he slapped me with a priority delivery first

thing. Someone promised their soul *and* body." He leaned back in his chair, shaking his head. "Souls are easy to wrangle to their fate. Bodies fight back."

Holy hell. His ears rang, the pressure in the room increasing until he thought he'd suffocate under the intensity.

"Here's your order, Mike." Destiny sashayed toward their table with a white pastry box in her hands. "I put a couple extra in, free of charge, since Richard keeps eating them all." She set the box on the table and rested a hand on Mike's shoulder.

A cooling sensation spread to his chest, and he was able to breathe again. "Who's the priority? What's their name?"

Asher fished his phone from his pocket and swiped the screen. "Crimson Oliver." His brow furrowed. "Isn't she the witch you've been after? Did you make this deal?"

"Fuck." He raked his hands through his hair. "Satan's balls. Fuck. Fuck! Fuck me with a cattle prod. Shit!"

Destiny recoiled, and Asher slowly returned his phone to his pocket. "I'm gonna take that as a yes."

"You can't take her." He slammed his hand on the table. His deal-sealing, life-fucking hand. "It was an accident. She didn't mean it. *I* didn't mean it."

"Oh, Mike." Destiny laced her fingers together and tilted her head. "You've got a rather aggressive way of showing it, but you love her, don't you?"

"With all my heart." And the organ was currently being ripped from his chest and shredded into a thousand pieces. He looked at Asher. "You can't take her."

"Satan will have my balls on a platter if I don't."

"He's not collecting balls anymore."

"Then he'll have my head. C'mon, Mike, you know

how this works. If I don't do my job, I might as well jump in the tarpits myself and save his minions the trouble."

Mike drummed his fingers on the table. This wasn't happening. He wouldn't allow it to happen. Crimson was the kindest, sweetest, gentlest soul he'd ever met. Satan would tire of her within a week, call her useless, and toss her aside like a charred appendix.

But Mike was the Devil's favorite advocate for a reason. Back in the day, there wasn't a deal he couldn't seal. It was time he brought out the big guns and showed Satan what a demon could do.

"I know you've got a job to do, but I guarantee she'll be off your list within an hour." He stood and grabbed the box of cakes. "I'm going to drop these off with Katrina, let her know what's happening, and then I'm going to pay the Devil a visit."

Asher nodded. "What are you going to do?"

Heat flashed in Mike's eyes. "I'm going to make him an offer he can't refuse."

Crimson looked everywhere for her demon. When she couldn't find him at work or at the bar he frequented, she snuck upstairs to his apartment, but it was empty. Her heart pounded in her throat as she made her way back to her building, but a sinking sensation threatened to pull the damn thing out through her ass if she didn't find him soon.

Something was wrong. Very, *very* wrong.

Inside her apartment, she set a blank canvas on an easel and squirted a blob of red paint on her palette. Brush in hand, she closed her eyes, willing the goddess to speak through her art and offer her a solution—or at least a hint—for this fiasco.

Her core tingled, the energy around her growing palpable as she waited for inspiration, but no images formed in her mind. The sound of someone clearing their throat made her jump, and as she opened her eyes to take in the form of a woman floating next to her, she squealed and fell backward onto her butt.

Sharp pain shot up her spine as her rear-end met wood, and the palette skidded across the floor. Crimson gasped at the ethereal beauty of the goddess, with her long dark hair flowing over her shoulders, almost floating as if she were underwater. She had sharp features, fair skin, and she wore a deep burgundy medieval-style gown.

Crimson opened her mouth, but the only words she could form were, "Holy shit."

The goddess suppressed a smile. "Is that any way to greet a deity?"

"I'm sorry." She scrambled to her feet and curtsied, squeezing her eyes shut and opening them again, not believing her vision. No one *saw* the goddess. *Jesus Christ on a bicycle.* "To what do I owe the honor of your presence?"

"You were trying to reach me, were you not?"

"Well, yeah, but we usually communicate through…" She held up the brush still clutched in her hand and shrugged.

The goddess smiled. "The man from hell has finished you. Your powers are fully unbound, and you can now use magic to your greatest potential."

"Yeah, about that…" She tossed the brush aside and clasped her hands together. "I didn't mean to sell my soul. I don't want to die."

"Who said anything about death?"

"How else will I meet Satan…the man from hell?"

The goddess tilted her head. "The Devil has nothing to do with your prophecy, child. The ability to channel my magic is rare and only granted to those who truly desire it, who truly desire to do good. Your demon has helped you realize your potential."

Crimson's mouth dropped open. Her demon? Mike was the man from hell? "I don't understand."

The goddess sighed. "You had accepted your incomplete magic. Your demon helped you realize you wanted more. When you truly believed, in your heart, that you deserved your full potential, the final piece of your power was unbound. You have access to my magic now."

"Oh, no." Crimson stumbled backward until the backs of her legs met the sofa, and she plopped onto the cushion.

"Do you not accept your full potential?" She lifted a hand. "I can take it away."

"I want it. I accept it." She looked into the goddess' emerald eyes. "But I accidentally sold my soul to the Devil."

The goddess nodded as if this wasn't new information. Crimson mentally smacked herself upside the head. Of course it wasn't. She was a goddess…all-knowing, duh.

"When you get there, find your line, and you will be saved."

Crimson scrunched her brow. "Find my line? What do you mean?"

The goddess pressed her palms together. "This is your first prophecy, child. Your demon is in peril, about to make a grave mistake. When you get to Satan's domain, find your line, and you will be saved."

"Do you have to be so cryptic? I mean, if I'm one of the few who can channel your magic and actually *see* you, maybe you can be a little more direct in your prediction delivery? What mistake? What line?"

With an amused grin, the goddess bowed her head and disappeared in a cloud of shimmering gold.

"Holy mother of glitter bombs." Crimson shot to her feet. What grave mistake was Mike about to make? Her stomach soured. She could think of several, and none of them boded well for his soul or their relationship.

She had to find *him* first, whatever the line was second. If she could keep him from making his grave mistake, maybe they could both be saved. When she tried his number, the call went straight to voicemail again, so she darted out the door and ran down the stairs.

Sharp pain sliced through Crimson's knuckles as she pounded on Sophie's door. As it swung open, her friend smiled. "Hey! Did you get it all worked out?"

"I can't find him." Her voice caught on the lump in her throat. "He's not answering his phone. He won't return my texts."

"He's probably licking his wounds. I'm sure he'll call you back. Wanna come in?" She opened the door wider, revealing her entire group of friends. Her fiancé, Trace, sat in the recliner, and her vampire friends Jane, Ethan, and Gaston occupied the sofa. "We were playing Cards Against Humanity. It's so much funnier when you're not actually human."

Crimson followed her into the living room. "Trace, you're friends with Mike. Will you text him and make sure he's okay?" If he was simply ignoring her calls, she might not be too late.

"Sure." Trace grabbed his phone and sent a text. The

phone pinged, and he rubbed his beard, squinting at the screen. "It says the message was undeliverable."

Oh no. She sank onto the arm of the couch, the weight of her ominous feeling making it impossible to stand. "Oh, Mike. What did you do?"

"It's Thursday, isn't it?" Trace asked.

"What does that matter?" Crimson chewed her bottom lip. It could have been midnight on a leap year. It wouldn't have changed the fact that Mike was missing, and her gut was telling her he'd done something rash to save her soul. His grave mistake.

"He goes to his HA meetings on Thursday nights. I bet he turned his phone off."

Sophie rubbed her arm. "That's probably it, hon. Try not to worry."

"Hold up." Jane rose to her feet and parked her hands on her hips. "Sophie said something about you maybe accidentally selling your soul. Is that true?"

Crimson made a face at Sophie. She should have known the news would travel fast when she confided in her. Then again, she never asked her to keep it a secret. "Yes. He said he was going to fix it, and I'm afraid he might have done something stupid. I just spoke to the goddess, and she said he was going to make a 'grave mistake.' I have to find him."

"Fuck trying not to worry," Jane said. "If I were you, I'd march my ass down to that meeting and drag him out by his balls."

Trace shook his head. "They won't let you in. I picked him up from a meeting once, and they had a guard posted at the end of the hall. I had to wait outside."

Finding him was more important than anything he could be doing at that meeting. Who knew what kind of power the other demons had? What if his mistake was enlisting the help of someone awful? Or worse, damning someone innocent? Crimson raised her eyebrows, glancing at each of her friends. "They can't stop all of us."

Gaston grinned, showing fang. "I do love smashing parties. Count me in."

Ethan stood. "It's *crashing* parties, and if Jane's in, so am I."

"You know I'm down." Jane took his hand and nodded at Crimson. "Let's go get your man and save your soul."

This right here was exactly why she'd half-joked about selling her soul in the first place. These people—her friends—meant everything to her, and if she had to leave New Orleans because she challenged the high priestess…

"Thanks, y'all. Let's go." She could worry about the what-ifs later. Right now, she needed to stop Mike before he did anything stupid.

When they arrived at the Priscilla St. James Community Center, only four cars occupied the parking lot. Most of the lights in the squat brown building were off, and the night air hung silent, except for the squawking of a crow sitting atop a light pole.

"Why is no one here?" Crimson's words created a fog in the chilly air.

Trace nodded toward a side entrance and led the way. "The place used to be packed at this time, but when the HA moved their meetings here, the other organizations slowly rescheduled theirs to different times. The humans may not understand or even believe in supes, but their instincts keep them as far away from the remnants of hell as they can get."

"And here I presumed they were all dumb as door-knockers," Gaston said.

"Watch it, buddy." Jane shook a finger at him. "I used to be human not too long ago."

"Hence my presumption." He arched a brow, and Jane stuck out her tongue.

They entered the building and made a left, but a human security guard blocked their way. Correction—the guy looked more like a mercenary than a rent-a-cop. He wore a black t-shirt with the sleeves ripped off to make room for his massive biceps, and two pistols were holstered at his sides, with a Bowie knife strapped to his thigh.

The soldier-for-hire crossed his arms and widened his stance. "You'll have to wait outside. This is a private meeting."

"It's an emergency." Crimson stepped toward him, but he didn't move. "I need to see Mike Cortez. Is he in there?"

"You'll have to wait outside," he growled.

"The hell we will." Crimson raised her hands and whispered a telekinesis incantation—since she could channel the goddess now and all—and the guy lifted from the ground, slamming back against the wall.

As Jane looked into his eyes and activated her vampire glamour, his face fell slack, his arms dropping to his sides, a bit of drool running from his mouth.

"What did you do to him?" Sophie gaped at the man.

"He'll be fine." Jane stepped back, eyeing the guy, and lifted his arm, letting it swing as she dropped it. "He might be limp all over for a while, but he can go a day or two without getting it up. Serves him right for trying to get in the way of love. Guys, why don't you stay here and babysit?"

Ethan chuckled. "Whatever you say, dear."

With hurried strides, Crimson burst through the door, and every head in the room swiveled to look at her. The demons sat in chairs arranged in a circle like it was some sort of group therapy session. She scanned the faces, but Mike wasn't among them.

"Can we help you?" A woman with dark hair swept into a ponytail and a nametag that read "Katrina" stood and slinked toward them.

Crimson glimpsed the nametags of the other demons: Richard, Sarah, Mark. They all had the most common human names imaginable. Where were the Beelzebubs and Amdusiases?

"Why do they all look so normal?" Sophie whispered.

"Maybe because they're recovering?" Why Crimson expected horns and hellfire, she had no clue. Mike was nothing like the stereotypical demon, so why should these people be?

Katrina had the look of a soccer mom, but with her fluid, graceful steps, she moved like a dancer—either ballet or exotic. "A witch, a werewolf, and a vampire. Are you looking for a demon to make a complete set?"

"We're looking for Mike. Have you seen him?" Her hands trembled, and she was tempted to slap the smirk off the demon's face.

Katrina's eyes widened. "You wouldn't happen to be Crimson, would you?"

Her pulse thrummed. "Yes. Why?"

Katrina licked her lips, and though Crimson didn't swing that direction, something about the woman screamed sex appeal. "I can see why he did it. You are scrumptious, aren't you? Tell me…" The demon rubbed her neck and tilted her head, her lids fluttering as if she enjoyed her own touch. "Is Mike as virile as I imagine him to be? I haven't sampled him myself—I'm fasting."

Crimson narrowed her eyes, trying to ignore the growing desire to plant her fist in the woman's face. Mike was *her* man. "You're a succubus, aren't you?"

Katrina recoiled, peeling back her lips and hissing as her eyes turned molten red. Jane stepped forward, hissing back, curling her hands into claws. Between a succubus and a vampire, her money was on Jane, but as Sophie growled low in her throat, the other demons in the room stood. They didn't move toward them, but as their eyes took on a red glow, the energy in the room grew palpable.

Crimson gripped Sophie's and Jane's arms. "These aren't good odds, ladies. Cool it."

As her friends stood down, Katrina inclined her chin. "Mike's in hell. He's going to trade his soul for yours."

"What?" The room spun, and she clutched her head, the nagging bad feeling she'd had all afternoon coming true. "He can't do that. He said the deal might not have taken. He was going to find someone else. He…"

Katrina crossed her arms. "Oh, it took."

"No." Crimson grabbed her phone and dialed Mike's number again. She couldn't let him do this. She could help him find a willing witch—or her *line*, whatever the hell that was. They could do it together. "Pick up."

"There's no mundane cell reception in hell." Katrina turned and slinked back to the circle of chairs.

"Seriously?" Jane gaped. "Why not?"

Katrina shrugged. "It's hell. Duh."

"I have to save him." She looked at Katrina. "How do I get to the underworld?"

"Simple. Just open a portal and hop through. Oh, wait. You're a witch; you can't open portals to the underworld. I guess you'll have to wait until you die." She laughed, and the other demons joined in, creating a discord of ominous, out-of-tune music. The soundtrack to a horror movie.

"Can one of you take me?"

Silence descended over the cacophony, and fear filled the demons' eyes. "Not a chance," Katrina said. "We left hell for a reason, and we are not going back."

"We'll pay you," Jane said. "Name your price."

"There's not enough money in the world to make going back there worth it." Katrina sank into her chair and crossed her legs. "Good luck, ladies. Now, if you'll excuse us."

Crimson's heart sank, a suffocating sensation pressing on her chest as Sophie wrapped an arm around her shoulders and guided her out of the meeting room. This couldn't be the end. Mike didn't get to just take her place without consulting her. That wasn't how relationships worked.

"How did it go?" Concern filled Ethan's gaze.

As Jane moved toward him, she snapped her fingers in the mercenary's face, and the guy blinked, coming back to himself. "You'll have to wait outside." He crossed his thick arms over his chest.

"Yeah, yeah. We're going." Jane led the group out the door and into the parking lot. "We need to figure out a way to bust into hell."

"I beg your pardon?" Gaston looked at them like they were crazy.

"The recovering demons are too scared to take me there." Crimson chewed her bottom lip, an idea forming in her mind. "Maybe I can summon another demon. One who's not recovering." She'd have to delve into the world of black magic to do it, but if it meant saving Mike's soul, she'd do anything. "I'm sure I can find a spell online." But what would the goddess think of her using her newfound powers for evil?

"Hold on." Trace held up his hands. "What do you think you're going to do once you get there?"

"Kick ass and take names, of course." Jane crossed her arms.

"That's right." Sophie fisted her hands on her hips. "We're going to show them who's boss."

Trace chuckled. "The three of you are going to fight Satan?"

"The six of us," Sophie said. "You're going to help, right?"

Crimson shook her head. "We can't fight the Devil. You saw how scared those demons were at the mere mention of returning to hell."

"At least one of you is making sense." Trace took Sophie's hand. "Mike is one of my best friends, and I will do anything to help him. But busting into hell without a plan is going to land us all in hot water. Literally."

"Mike said Satan loves to gamble. We're going to have to figure out a way to outsmart him." Crimson wrapped her arms around herself. "And if we can't do that, I'll give myself up. I'm the one who offered my soul. Mike shouldn't have to suffer for my careless words."

Jane wiped a tear from her eye. "That's true love right there."

That's exactly what it was. She was in love with Mike, and there was no way—in hell or on Earth—she'd let the Devil have him. "I have to do it alone. I won't risk your souls too. Let me find a summoning spell." She opened the web browser on her phone.

"This is the worst idea I've heard since Miss Jane thought a vampire could sustain herself on rare steak," Gaston said. "Recovering demons are one thing, but you are talking about summoning a creature straight from hell. He'll devour you before he'll help you."

Crimson arched a brow. "Do you have a better idea?"

The vampire crossed his arms, inclining his chin. "Why don't you find a reaper? They cross between hell and Earth on a daily basis. Surely one of them could get you in."

"Can you summon a reaper?" Sophie asked. "How will we even find one?"

Trace let out a heavy sigh. "I know where to find one. Let's go."

CHAPTER ELEVEN

"Michael, my friend." Satan pushed back from his desk and propped his ankle on his knee, steepling his fingers. His iridescent red suit caught the light of the fire licking up toward the ceiling in his office, making it shimmer as if the garment itself were magical. Glittery flames adorned his black tie, and silver skull cufflinks glinted as he moved. "Have you come to deliver my witch yourself?"

Straightening his spine, Mike swallowed the bile from the back of his throat and approached the desk. "There's been a mistake. You can't have Crimson."

A slow smile curved his lips, and as he flicked his wrist, a scroll appeared in his hands. "The Devil doesn't make mistakes." He unrolled the parchment. "The contract is complete. I love her name, by the way. My favorite color."

"*I* made the mistake." His hands curled into fists, and he fought the urge to yank the contract from Satan's hands, tearing it to shreds.

"You're my advocate, an extension of myself. If I don't

make mistakes, neither do you. Are you sure you want to give up that kind of perfection, by the way? I'm more than willing to let you stay on if you've decided freedom isn't all it's cracked up to be."

"She was joking. She didn't really want to sell her soul."

He scanned the contract. "It says right here she was only half-joking. Half-joking means half-serious, and that's good enough for me." He tossed the scroll onto his desk, and it disappeared in a puff of red smoke.

"Excuse me, sir?" Esmerelda, his temporary assistant, slipped through the door and stood against the wall. "Your ten o'clock is here."

"Thank you, dear. I'll just be a moment." Satan stood and strolled around the desk. "What do you say, Michael? Will you remain on the winning team, or do you want your measly freedom when my witch arrives?"

"I want more time. I want you to redact that contract and give me the remainder of my month to find you a suitable assistant. Crimson was raised by an angel. Believe me, she's not wicked enough to fulfill this role."

"She'll be plenty wicked by the time I'm done with her. No deal."

The door thudded behind Esmerelda as she scurried out of the room, and Mike's heart threatened to beat out of his chest. "Please, Satan. I can find someone better. I can—"

"I said, 'no deal!'" His voice boomed, echoing off the chamber walls.

"I love her!" He clamped his mouth shut. He didn't mean to say it out loud. The Devil didn't give a damn about love, but Mike's heart had been ripped from his chest, and Satan clutched it in his fist.

The Devil paused, and eerie quiet stuffed the room like cotton. Clasping his hands behind his back, he strolled in a circle around Mike, his gaze raking up and down his form before he stopped in front of him, face to face. "Well, why didn't you say so?"

Mike ground his teeth, cursing himself for letting his true feelings slip. "Does it make a difference?"

"In her fate? No. But it does make the entire ordeal much more enjoyable for me. My favorite advocate won his freedom by damning the woman he loves. It simply can't get better than this."

No. He would not let this happen. Crimson was right; he should have trusted her from the beginning. If he'd have told her upfront what kind of magic he had, she could have decided for herself if she wanted to get involved with him. Instead, he'd resorted to his demonic ways—not truly tricking her, but withholding essential information she needed to make an informed decision about him.

Who was he kidding? He didn't belong topside. No demon did. "Take me instead. I'll be your assistant."

Satan laughed. "I've always had a witch."

"So? Times change, and so should you. I've got some ideas on how to liven this place up, and we can start with getting rid of that horrid nineties Halloween soundtrack."

The Devil crossed his arms. "I happen to like horrid."

"C'mon, Satan. You lost me in a *poker game*. Now's your chance to save face. Show everyone you can't be fooled. Set Crimson free, and take me instead."

The Devil's eyes narrowed, a look of confusion contorting his features. "You love this witch so much you'd give up your freedom for all eternity?"

"Yes, I do." He didn't even have to think about his answer. He'd do anything for her.

"I stand corrected. It can get better." A diabolical laugh vibrated in the devil's chest. "All right, Michael, but I don't want you as my assistant. You'll be my favorite advocate again, and your first job will be to find my new assistant. No more games. Crimson goes free; you stay. A soul for a soul. Do we have a deal?"

Mike's palm burned, and heat flashed in his eyes as he stretched his arm toward the Devil, shaking his hand and sealing his fate for eternity.

———

"You have to, Asher. It's the only way to save him." Crimson gripped the reaper's arm and pleaded with her gaze. Trace stood behind her, along with the rest of her friends, and Asher glared at the werewolf.

"He's going to kill me if I do. You realize that, right?"

Trace shrugged. "I thought reapers were immortal."

"He'll throw me in the tarpits. Or even worse, he'll have me reassigned to Alaska." He shuddered. "I can't stand snow."

"But you can do it, right?" Crimson begged. "You can get me into hell?"

With a heavy sigh, Asher tugged his phone from his pocket and swiped at the screen. "Crimson Oliver. Soul and body. High priority." He turned the device toward her, and she glimpsed her name along with several others. Hers was the only priority and the only one that required the body be delivered as well. "Mike asked me for an hour. It's only been fifty-five minutes."

"Good. Then I still have five minutes to stop him."

Sophie put a hand on her shoulder. "Are you sure you want to do this, hon?"

"I'd rather spend an eternity in hell than five minutes on Earth knowing Mike is suffering because of me. Besides…" She shrugged. "I'm channeling the goddess now. Between my magic, Mike's bargaining power, and finding my line, I'm sure we'll strike a deal that makes us all happy."

"Just so you know," Asher said, "I can get you into hell, but I've never tried bringing anyone back out. I'm not sure I can."

"Just get me in. I'll worry about getting out." *If I get the chance.*

"Crimson…" Jane stepped forward, pulling her into a bear hug. "You got this. I know you do."

"Thanks." She stood next to Asher and took his hand, her heart threatening to beat right out of her chest. "I'll see you on the flip side."

With a wave of his arm, Asher ripped a hole in reality and yanked Crimson through. They landed on a giant boulder inside a massive cave with red and black crystals coating the walls. A raging river, black as the midnight sky, cut through the rocks, blocking their access to the mainland in the distance.

"Don't tell me I have to swim for it." A nervous giggle escaped her throat as she peered at the steaming swirl of water below, and a tortured scream pierced through the sound of the rapids. She shuddered.

"All topside souls enter the Devil's domain here, but only those who've been invited can cross. If you fall in, you'll be boiled alive for eternity. The Greeks called this the River Styx."

She inched back, away from the ledge. "What's it called now?"

He grinned. "The River Styx."

Crimson nodded. "If it's not broke…" A small boat approached from the mainland, and Crimson squeezed her eyes shut, opening them again to find the same odd image. About the size and shape of a gondola, the boat cut across the river, slicing through the current, calming the waters around the vessel and making it look like it floated on a serene lake. "Is that our ride?"

"Hm?" Asher had been staring at his phone, but he glanced up at her question. "Yeah. This is weird."

"What's weird?"

"Your name is gone." He flashed the phone screen toward her. "You've been struck from the list."

"Because I'm here, right? You did your job and delivered my body and soul to hell."

"That's not how it usually works. You have to be processed first. How else would Satan know you've arrived?"

"He's not all-knowing?"

Asher shook his head.

"Maybe he's watching? I am supposed to be his personal assistant."

"Asher, what have you brought for us today?" The man piloting the gondola parked it alongside the rock, and it floated out of the water to their level. "You're a brave one promising your body too, young lady. Don't get on Satan's bad side; I hear torture of the flesh is almost as bad as that of the soul."

His brow furrowed, Asher shook his head and shoved his phone into his pocket. "This is Charon."

The man had messy, poofy brown hair—with his

ghostly white skin and deep purple circles ringing his eyes, he most likely didn't give a damn about appearances—but the way it stuck up in the back and framed his face made it look like it belonged on a forty-five-year-old soccer mom with permanent resting bitch face.

Crimson bit her tongue, holding in a giggle. "Karen? As in 'I want to speak to the manager' Karen?"

"My name is Cha*ron*, child, and if you want to cross safely, you'd best hold your tongue."

"I'm sorry. You're right; that was rude of me." And insulting to the Karens of the world. "I'm a little nervous to be here."

"As you should be," Cha*ron* said.

"Lighten up. If you'd ever been topside, you'd know how funny that was." Asher dropped two silver coins in the man's hand and looked at Crimson. "Charon is my great-great-great-grandpa."

"You make me sound old when you say it like that." He placed the coins in the pocket of his long black robe.

"You're ancient." Asher gestured to the boat, and Crimson stepped inside. As soon as the reaper set foot in the craft, it lowered into the water, and Charon paddled them to the mainland. Though, saying he paddled was a stretch. The boat seemed to accelerate of its own accord while Charon moved the oar for show.

She started to ask what the man's purpose was if the ferry worked on its own, but spending eternity boiling alive in a raging river wasn't the slightest bit appealing. It was best not to piss off a man who could send her to a fate worse than death.

When the boat docked, Asher took her hand and helped her ashore. The tortured screams grew louder, followed by a pained howl and then a screech.

"Is Satan torturing a werewolf?" Her hands trembled, so she fisted them. She could not show weakness if she planned to bargain with the Devil himself.

Asher chuckled. "It's an audio track I bought as a gag gift back in the nineties. We had a white elephant party for Halloween, and Satan loved it. He plays it at all the entrances to intimidate people."

"At least he's got a sense of humor." She found a massive sign that read "To Processing" with a long line of people standing under it. Some were dressed in suits and formalwear, while others wore jeans, workout clothes, and even pajamas. They all stood stagnant, facing forward, not conversing and definitely not smiling.

"I guess that's the line I'm supposed to find." She moved toward it, though how it could save her, she had no clue. Maybe the goddess meant a metaphorical line?

Asher caught her hand. "That's the general processing line. You're a priority delivery, so I have to escort you straight to Satan's palace."

She looked at her hand nestled in Asher's and then at the stagnant line of people. It hadn't moved a single inch since she arrived. "Are there more lines in hell, because the goddess was specific. She said I have to find my line and I'll be saved."

"I don't know what goes on inside the palace, but I promise general processing is not where you want to be." He nodded at the mass of people. "See that guy with a black football jersey?

"Yes." He stood in the sixth position from the end.

"I dropped him off last Tuesday."

She gasped. "The palace it is, then. Lead the way."

As she followed the reaper on the path to the palace, she took in the jagged, rocky surroundings. From what she could see, hell appeared to be an enormous cave with soaring ceilings and ominous walls that seemed to loom over the inhabitants, threatening to crush them at any second.

And the atmosphere… If the intense smell of sulfur wasn't enough to choke her, the thickness of the air made August in the French Quarter feel like a windy winter day.

Sweat beaded on her forehead and dripped down her back, the heat and humidity winding her curls into tight spirals. "Is it always so hot here?"

"You get used to it." He paused twenty feet from a massive lava-filled moat and pressed his hand against some type of access device. A thick metal bridge slid across the channel, and Crimson peered upward at the colossal palace.

Made of obsidian, the castle towered into what would have been the sky if hell had one. Instead, its spires disappeared into the darkness of the vaulted cave, and the glass walls glinted in the firelight from the molten stream surrounding it. "Wow."

"Impressive, isn't it?"

"It looks like it should belong to a Disney villain. I could see Maleficent living here." She followed Asher across the bridge and stopped outside the front door.

"Don't compare the Devil to any kind of Hollywood bad guy, especially the ones from the James Bond series. He thinks he's original and that the movie villains are fashioned after him." He pressed a buzzer and stepped back. "Spend enough time around here, and you know it's the other way around. Ask him about the sharks with lasers on their foreheads. That's his favorite story to tell."

"Sharks with lasers?" This was going to be a quick in

and out operation. She definitely did *not* want to ask the Devil about sharks. "You're coming in, right?"

Asher held up his hands. "I haven't been summoned, so this is as far as I'm allowed to go."

Icy panic flushed through her veins. "How will I know where to go? This place is massive."

"Just follow the signs to Satan's offices. Good luck!" He turned on his heel and disappeared. Literally disappeared, like into thin air.

"I'd love to learn that trick."

A speaker on the wall next to the door crackled, and a woman's voice said, "State your name and purpose, please."

She leaned toward the microphone. "Crimson Oliver. I believe I'm supposed to be Satan's new assistant."

A *thunk* sounded as the lock disengaged, and the ginormous glass door swung open. Crimson's heart leapt into her throat as she stepped through the threshold.

Her heels clicked on the black marble floor, and she stared in awe at the gleaming red spires jutting up from the floor to the soaring ceiling. The palace was enormous, with winding staircases leading up to who knew where and dozens of arches that opened into hallways darting out in all directions.

Any one of them could have been "the line" she was supposed to find, and she didn't have a clue where to go from here. She took two more steps into the grand foyer, and a row of flames shot up along the wall to her left, the heat blasting her like she stood too close to a pizza oven. Could that be the line she was looking for? *How the hell am I supposed to know?*

As she turned her face away from the fire, a sign illuminated above an archway. Then another sign lit up, and another, until every passage revealed the location it led to. She could go to the stalagmite gardens, the lava pools, the decontamination chamber…

She shivered. What on Earth would a person in hell need to decontaminate from? The widest archway held a sign that read "To Satan's Chambers." She moved toward it, but hesitated. *You're not seeing any lines here, Crim, so you might as well go straight to the top.*

Her footsteps echoed as she made her way down the dimly lit hallway. Lanterns engulfed in blood-red glass provided the only light, and no side hallways jutted from the long, narrow, winding corridor she ventured down.

She walked for what felt like hours, or maybe it was only seconds. Time seemed to lose its meaning here, and as the hallway made a sharp bend to the right, it spilled out into a great chamber drenched in red.

Red velvet chairs lined one wall, and heavy red drapes hung from the darkened windows. A woman with a short, dark pixie cut sat at an onyx desk near a massive set of wooden double doors, and Crimson's breath caught at the sight of her. With dark skin, a soft jaw and delicate nose, the woman was the spitting image of Crimson's birth mother.

She couldn't stop her feet from carrying her forward, bursting into a run as she crossed the chamber. Skidding to a stop in front of the desk, she held her breath as the woman looked up from her computer and held her gaze.

"Mom?" Her voice sounded tiny in the massive room.

The woman blinked, a look of disbelief flashing in her eyes as she rose to her feet and strode around the desk. "Crimson? What are you doing here? You're saved. You shouldn't have come." She clutched her shoulders and then pulled her into a tight hug. "But I'm so happy to see you."

Pressure mounted in Crimson's eyes as she hugged her mother, the familiar scent of cloves mixing with the sulfurous aroma of hell. "Why are you here, Mom? Do you work for the Devil?"

She pulled back, cupping Crimson's face in her hands. "I'm filling in until he finds a new assistant."

"That's supposed to be me, but Mike's going to trade his soul for mine."

Her mom shook her head. "Oh, sweetheart, he already made the deal. You need to leave. Go back to Earth before Satan finds you here."

"What? No! No, he didn't. That's not how this is supposed to work. The goddess told me to come here, to find my line, and I'll be saved. Mike is supposed to be free."

Her mom's eyes widened. "You…spoke to the goddess? Directly?"

"Yes, she came into my loft while I was trying to channel her. She told me I don't have to paint to channel her anymore, that Mike—bless his soul—and his demonic power to bring out my greatest desire finished unlocking the last of my magic. I can channel straight from the goddess herself now."

Her mouth fell open as she froze, stunned. "The man from hell will finish you…"

"The prophecy was talking about Mike. It didn't mean I would sell my soul—that was an accident. I'd been raised to accept myself for who I was—an incomplete witch. Mike made me realize what I really wanted…to be whole. I can't let Satan have him, Mom. I need to find my line."

"Your line?" Clutching the edge of the desk, she lowered herself down as if afraid her knees wouldn't hold her. "I believe your line is me."

CHAPTER TWELVE

"You are never to return to New Orleans again." Satan leaned back in his chair and laced his fingers behind his head, spreading his elbows wide. "I'm reassigning you to Los Angeles until you forget about your witch and rediscover your demonic nature."

That'll never happen. Mike bowed his head. "Are you sure you want to send someone with my experience to the Devil's playground? People beg to sell their souls there every day."

"That's exactly why I want you to go. You'll be making deals faster than a succubus can get laid. More often too."

A blast of hot air wafted in as the double doors swung open. Mike spun around to find Crimson standing at the entrance, her hands fisted on her hips, her head held high. She wore a tight black t-shirt and onyx leggings that not only showed off her curves but also made her look like she was ready to kick someone's ass. That or do yoga, but he was betting by the look on her face that ass-kicking was on the agenda. *Uh-oh.*

Her dark spiral curls flowed down to her shoulders,

and she strode toward them with a confidence in her gait he'd never seen before. Gone was the broken witch afraid to use her powers for fear of screwing up. Crimson had gone from bad witch to badass, and he'd never loved her more.

Mike's mouth hung open, so he snapped it shut and scrambled for something to say. His new deal with Satan was binding. She was a free woman, yet she'd somehow managed to travel through hell, straight into the Devil's lair to find him.

"I demand you release him." Her voice was strong and confident, and as she stopped next to Mike, she rested a hand on his shoulder and kissed his cheek. "Hey, babe. Sorry I freaked out on you. I'm here to make things right."

"How did you…?" He couldn't finish the sentence. His brain hadn't caught up with the fact that the woman he loved was standing next to him…in hell.

"Your reaper friend brought me."

"Just who the hell do you think you are?" Satan clasped his hands on his desk. "And how did you get past my assistant?"

Crimson cocked her head. "Whoa. The Devil really does wear Prada. Did you start before or after the movie?"

Satan's eyes turned molten red, and a low growl rumbled in his chest. Mike wouldn't have been surprised if steam shot out of his ears too. "Before, naturally," the Devil replied coolly. "The humans mimic me; it's *never* the other way around." He pressed a button on his phone. "Esmerelda, remove this witch from my office immediately. Esmerelda?"

When she didn't respond, he mashed the buttons five more times and then swiped the phone from his desk, sending it crashing to the ground. Rising to his feet, he straightened his shoulders and strolled around the desk, his lips curving into a sneer. "Let me guess. You're the witch Michael gave up his freedom for. Crimson, isn't it?"

She swallowed hard and slipped her hand into Mike's. "I am, and I'm here to demand you release him. Your deal is with me. I'm your new assistant."

"Crimson, no." Surely she wasn't here to take his place. "I've already made a new deal. You're free. You shouldn't have come."

"But I *want* to be here." She looked at the Devil. "Let him go, and I'll fulfill my end of the deal. I'll be your assistant for the rest of eternity, or until you get tired of me. I hear there's quite a turnaround for this position."

Footsteps pounded on the floor behind them as John, one of Satan's grunts, stormed into the room. Standing nearly seven feet tall, the barrel-chested guard demon had skin the color of clay bricks. "I got your call, sir. How can I assist?"

The Devil pressed his lips together like he was fighting a smile. "This *witch* broke into my office, and I'm—"

Before he could finish his sentence, John lunged at Crimson. Mike started toward the demon, but Crimson threw up her hands and shouted, "Demon fat, you're now a cat."

John froze in mid-air, his eyes going wide a split second before he dropped to the floor and transformed into a fluffy white kitten.

He sat on his haunches, blinking at her and then at Satan. "Mew?" His meow sounded like a question, and Mike could only imagine what the poor fiend must have been thinking.

Crimson crossed her arms and turned to Satan. "I wouldn't advise siccing another dog on me. I doubt the

Devil wants an army of kittens. Imagine what it would do to your reputation."

"Crimson…" Mike tried to lace his voice with warning, but truth be told, Crimson impressed the hell out of him. Satan could make the biggest, baddest demon cower with nothing more than a pointed look, and this witch, *his witch*, just threatened to turn his entire legion feline.

For the first time in the eighty-some-odd-years Mike had known the Devil, he looked dumbfounded. Maybe a little impressed too. Stooping to the floor, Satan scooped John into his arms and returned to his chair, stroking the cat's back…again like a James Bond villain, though Mike didn't dare mention the similarity.

"Your magic is impressive." Satan grinned when the cat purred. "What's stopping me from keeping both of you? Mike did make a deal with me, and you stormed into my office unsummoned. I believe I've landed a new assistant and gotten my best advocate back on the same day."

"You don't want to do that." Crimson sank into the chair across from the Devil's desk, and Mike stood behind her, still unable to believe this was the same woman he left topside. "If you keep us both, then we'll be together. As much as I hate the heat down here, if I get to be with Mike, I'll be happy. So will he, right, babe?"

He sat in the chair next to her. "She's right. That's why you should send her home and let me find you someone else. Someone I can't stand."

"No." Crimson shook her head. "You should release Mike, grant him full freedom and return him to Earth. I'll stay here and be miserable without him."

Mike took her hand. "Crimson, you can't do this. I'm a demon; I'm *supposed* to live in hell. You need to get back up there, beat Rosemary, and save your coven. I know you can do it."

"Oh, I can beat her. I'm channeling magic straight from the goddess now, thanks to you. But I don't need to if I'm Satan's assistant. You go home. You belong up there."

"Well, well." Satan laid the cat in his lap and steepled his fingers, chuckling. "This is getting more and more fun. What to do? What to do?"

"Keep me," they both said in unison.

He couldn't let her do this. With her kind heart, she'd never survive in the underworld. "It was *my* mistake. I shouldn't have shaken your hand. I shouldn't have offered the deal. I didn't mean to damn you, Crimson. I love you. Please let this be the last thing I do to prove my love. Let me allow you to live."

Tears collected on her lower lids, and her bottom lip trembled. "Oh, Mike. That's the sweetest thing anyone has ever done for me. I love you too, and that's why *you* have to go. I said the words aloud. I agreed to the deal, so it's on me." She turned to the Devil. "Satan, what do you say? Send him topside, with one hundred percent freedom, and you can have me, a witch who can channel the magic of the goddess herself."

The Devil tapped a finger against his lips. "The goddess in what form?"

"All of them, though she visited me as Morrigan."

As Satan shot to his feet, the kitten tumbled to the floor with a *thunk*. It appeared that only those born feline always landed on their feet. "You have a deal." He jutted his hand toward Crimson, and before Mike could stop her, she shook, sealing the bargain.

His spine tingled, and then it snapped, the twenty-four-seven connection to the Devil dissolving like an all-night diner going out of business. He was free, and she…

"Crimson, what have you done?"

"I granted you your freedom." She smiled proudly. "Your greatest desire."

"My greatest desire is to spend the rest of my life with you. Now that will never happen."

"Don't be so sure." She winked and turned toward the entrance, where Esmerelda strutted in.

The temporary assistant stopped next to Crimson, who stood, grinning like she hadn't just promised Satan an eternity of servitude. The Devil rose and cut his gaze between the two women, his eyes calculating, and Mike stood because…well, everyone else was standing, so it seemed like the right thing to do.

"It's time for you to hold up your end of the bargain, Satan." Esmerelda rested a hand on Crimson's shoulder, and the Devil let out a long, slow, overly controlled breath, which meant he was pissed.

"This is cheating. You tricked me." Satan scooped the cat from the floor and ran his hand over its back. *Poor John. His buddies will never let him live this down.*

"It's not cheating at all," Crimson said. "You made a deal with me, but the deal you made with her is still binding."

"Would someone mind explaining what's going on?" Mike asked.

"Crimson is my daughter," Esmerelda glanced at Mike before casting a loving gaze at Crimson.

"She received a prophecy from the goddess that she *thought* meant I was going to sell my soul one day. So, on her death bed, she made her own deal with the Devil. She'd serve as a magic instructor for his demon/witch hybrids in exchange for a get-out-of-hell-free card for me whenever I needed it." Crimson wrapped an arm around her mom's shoulders. "And here we are, come full circle."

"Wait." Mike squeezed his eyes shut, trying to make his brain catch up with the events unfolding before him. "Even though I damned you, you would have been released because of the deal your mother made when you were a kid?"

"Yep. We had nothing to worry about."

He glanced between the two women. "Would have been nice if you'd told me that a couple of weeks ago."

"I just found out today." Crimson's smile was warmer than the flames licking the walls behind them. "I had no idea my mom was here."

Esmerelda nodded. "And you never told me what name you were looking for on the manifest when you were here before."

Mike shook his head. "I have got to get better at communicating."

They all looked at Satan, his molten eyes undulating as he observed their exchange. "I must say, I have respect for anyone who can pull one over on the Devil himself. Good show, all of you." He flicked his wrist dismissively. "You're both free. Esmerelda, you'll return to your teaching duties as soon as a permanent assistant is found."

"Mom, can't you come with us? Can we make another deal?"

"No more deals, sweetheart." She took her daughter's hands. "It's not a bad afterlife here, and Satan's not as bad as he pretends to be either." Esmerelda winked at the Devil, and unless Mike's eyes deceived him, he could have sworn he saw a blush spread across the Prince of the Underworld's cheeks.

The Devil sighed and cast a longing gaze toward Crimson. "I was looking forward to your magic. I don't know how I'll find an assistant as powerful as you. Are you sure you don't want to stay here with your mom?"

"Don't even think about it, Crimson," Esmerelda scolded. "You belong topside with that demon of yours. The prophecy stated it, so mote it be."

"I'm going to miss you, Mom." Crimson hugged Esmerelda, and then she stepped toward Mike, taking his hand. "Let's go home."

He pulled her to his chest, wrapping her in his arms and memorizing the way she felt against him. This amazing woman had traveled all the way to hell to save him. To be with him. *That* was true love.

"Oh!" She lifted her head from his shoulder. "Satan, I may know of someone who'd make a diabolical assistant. She's powerful too."

He dropped the cat on his desk. "I'm listening."

"Meet us topside day after tomorrow at three."

He tapped on his smart watch. "I'll be there with bells on."

"Hell's bells?"

He grinned. "Of course."

"Are you going to fix John?" Mike nodded toward the kitten swatting at a pen lying on the desk. "He's been humiliated long enough."

Crimson opened her mouth to speak, but Satan moved in front of the cat, blocking her spell. "Don't touch him. I rather like him this way."

CHAPTER THIRTEEN

The sun shone brightly in the cloudless afternoon sky as Crimson walked hand in hand with Mike toward the coven house. Sophie and Trace followed behind, and as they turned the corner, the house coming into view, a sense of pride washed over Crimson, lighting in her heart.

Massive ferns overflowing their pots hung from the eaves, and the deep blue paint on the exterior gave the witches' headquarters a welcoming façade.

Welcoming. That was something the coven *hadn't* been since Rosemary became high priestess six years ago. Things were about to change.

"I don't understand," Sophie said as they stopped on the sidewalk outside. "If the challenge starts at two, why did you tell Satan to come at three? Wouldn't it have been easier to let him talk to Rosemary beforehand so you don't even have to *do* the contest?"

"It would be easier." Crimson glanced through the great room window where the crowd was gathering. "But I've spent my entire life as a broken witch. They were nice to me because they felt sorry for me, and when a spell went wrong, no one was surprised. I need to prove—to them and to myself—that I don't need their sympathy anymore. That I deserve to be high priestess because the goddess deemed it so."

"Gotcha." Sophie nodded. "You need to kick some witch ass and show them who's boss. Jane would have loved to see this."

Crimson smiled. "We can tell her all about it over drinks tonight."

Mike chuckled. "Are the boys invited?"

"You know it. I wouldn't have the confidence to win this challenge if it weren't for you." She kissed his cheek, and he swept her into his arms, spinning in a circle before lowering her feet to the ground and planting one on her lips.

Her body warmed as his strong arms held her, and when his tongue brushed hers, she detected a faint hint of angel food cake. Though he was no longer required to make deals for the Devil, recovering demons—even ones with one hundred percent freedom—still had demonic urges from time to time.

The cake helped to subdue his demon side, and that was fine, as long as it didn't tame his beast in the sheets. She was looking forward to some more of that action.

Trace cleared his throat. "Incoming."

Crimson reluctantly released Mike's lips and turned to find Asher striding toward them. Her stomach bubbled, the thought that Satan may have changed his mind turning it sour. "I hope you're not here to take one of us this time."

Asher laughed. "Nope. I'm here for the show. Anyone who knows Rosemary wants to see her get her ass kicked. I'm not late, am I?"

"You're right on time." Crimson led the way into the coven house. The murmur of voices grew louder as they paced down the hall toward the great room, the plush green runner on the floor masking the sounds of their footsteps.

She rested her hand on the knob and turned to her friends. "Nothing like a grand entrance, right?" Twisting the knob, she flung open the door and strutted inside like she owned the place—because in an hour, this coven would be hers.

A hush fell across the crowd as Crimson paced to the center of the challenge arena, and her friends found seats among the other witches.

Rosemary stomped forward, her permanent scowl even more defined as she glared at Crimson before gesturing to her friends. "Who are they?"

"Witnesses." Crimson inclined her chin. "You may have every witch in the coven under your thumb, but you can't fool my friends. They're here to make sure you play fair."

"And to watch you get your ass kicked," Asher called from the second row.

Rosemary grunted. "You brought a reaper to scare me? I know he can't do anything to me unless I'm called to the underworld. He's nothing but a slave to Satan."

Crimson fought a smile. "I have no need to intimidate you, Rosemary. I'm going to win this challenge fairly... and easily."

She snorted. "Riiight. Laila, let's get this over with. I don't want to miss *Dancing with the Stars* tonight."

Laila stepped into the arena wearing a long, burgundy robe trimmed in gold braided rope—the judgment robe—and lifted her hands in the air. "I call on the goddess to begin this rite and select our high priestess with justness and honor."

Her fingers sparkled with golden magic, and a fledgling witch in the back gasped and slumped into her mother's side. *Amateur.* As the air wavered around Laila's hands, the sparkles formed into words. The name of the first test. *Rejuvenation.*

Two witches wearing mauve robes shuffled in, each one carrying a dying miniature potted rose bush in her hands. They set the flowers on the tables, and Crimson and Rosemary approached their first test.

Crimson eyed her flower. To say it was dying was a stretch. This thing looked like a vegetarian vampire had sucked it dry and left it to wither on the asphalt in July. She touched a bud, and every damn leaf and dried-up petal—save for one—rained to the dirt. *Good job, Crim. Way to make things harder.*

Rosemary snickered, and when no one else laughed, she glared at the witches closest to her. When two of them forced out fake giggles, Rosemary smiled smugly. Crimson half-expected her to stick out her tongue too. It would've been fitting since the priestess was acting like a grade school bully.

"You must bring the flowers back to life," Laila said. "Your time starts now."

Crimson took a deep breath, shuffling through the spells in her mind. She settled on a twist of an incantation her mom used when she'd forgotten to water the ivy in the coffee shop. From the corner of her eye, she glimpsed the priestess' flower growing, the life returning to its petals before she'd even cast her spell.

She could do this. She had goddess magic now. "Delicate flower, it's time to show. In the name of the goddess, I ask you to grow."

As she aimed her magic toward the flower, she opened up, allowing the goddess to flow through her. The rose stem straightened, and then a new bud and leaves formed. Rosemary laughed and crossed her arms, her tiny rose completely revived.

Crimson opened her channel further, giving one more push of magic, and the flower bloomed. Then another bud popped up and bloomed. Then another. The small plant grew into a bush, and as the roots became more than the pot could hold, it shattered, spilling dirt over the table and eliciting startled squeals from the audience.

"That's my girl," Mike hollered from his seat in the back row, and Crimson's heart warmed. She smiled at him, and he mouthed the words *they all want you to win.*

Her lips parted on a quick inhale, and he nodded, pressing a hand to his chest to indicate he could feel their desire. The coven *wanted* her to win. They wanted to be rid of Rosemary as badly as she did.

"Looks like I win that round." Rosemary raised her hand, drawing the attention back to herself. "I got mine up faster."

"Maybe, but mine's bigger, and no matter what people say, size *does* matter." She winked at her demon. "I should know."

"Hell yeah!" Sophie shouted. When the other witches turned to look at her, she clamped her mouth shut and muttered, "Sorry."

"The goddess will determine the winner at the end of the challenge." Laila raised her hands again, and the next spell appeared in the air.

They went through the series of tests, each spell

becoming harder and more complex. Rosemary completed them all with ease, but Crimson hesitated on the first few. Her hands, slick with sweat, trembled as she mixed the potions. The priestess was faster at first, but as her confidence grew, Crimson caught up. The challenge was close, with no clear winner yet.

"The final test." Laila lifted her arms one last time, and the final spell illuminated the room. *Shapeshifting of Another Being*. Beneath the name of the spell came the words *Form of a cat and back to human*.

"Oh, you've got to be kidding me. This has to be rigged." Crimson parked her hands on her hips, cutting her gaze between Laila and Rosemary. The spell that landed her in hot water to begin with—the one incantation she hadn't practiced—was the final spell in the competition?

Rosemary laughed. "I hope you've got someplace to stay, because your banishment starts the moment this is done."

"Don't be so sure of yourself." Like Crimson could talk. She was the one lacking confidence at the moment.

Laila shook her head as if disappointed in their attempts at trash talk. "Who volunteers to be Rosemary's subject?" After a slight hesitation and some hard, audible swallows, several hands lifted in the audience.

"Amarillo, I choose you." The priestess smirked at Crimson. "What happens when she can't get a volunteer?"

"If no one is willing to be her subject, the test is forfeited, and the opponent will be declared winner of that spell." Laila closed her eyes, swaying slightly as if receiving a message from the great beyond. "Who volunteers to be Crimson's subject? It cannot be anyone with shapeshifting abilities."

Sophie, who had started to stand, sank into her chair. All the witches in the audience cast their gazes downward, which Crimson expected. Even if they trusted her to be able to change them back—and Crimson didn't even trust herself—going up against Rosemary would be suicide if she won.

"I volunteer as tribute." Mike stood and strode into the arena.

"Can you shapeshift?" Laila asked.

He stood next to Crimson. "Nope. That's not how my magic works."

"Demons are liars." Rosemary gave him a once-over with her gaze. "Unless he's willing to reveal his magic to the entire coven, he can't be trusted."

"No, Mike. You don't have to do that." Crimson scanned the crowd, but none of the witches would look at her. "Asher? Could you?"

"I'd love to, but reapers can shapeshift. Sometimes turning into a giant skeleton and wielding a scythe is the only way to convince people they're dead."

Crimson shook her head. "Let me call someone else. Demons never reveal their magic."

"The challenge is a timed trial," Laila said. "I'm afraid we only have ten minutes left."

"It's okay." Mike took her hand and flashed a reassuring smile. "If my magic scares people away, so be it. I've got you, and that's all that matters." He looked at the crowd. "I'm a recovering Devil's advocate. I used to make deals for Satan, but thanks to this amazing woman…" He wrapped an arm around Crimson's shoulders. "I'm free. I don't damn people anymore."

Rosemary's mouth dropped open. "You worked

directly for Satan? Where were you a month ago when I... Never mind."

Laila's eyes turned glassy as she channeled the goddess' decree. "He is telling the truth, and he may be used as her subject."

"Don't expect anyone in the coven to help you change him back when he gets stuck." Rosemary swept her gaze across the audience, driving the order home.

Crimson swallowed hard. Turning him into a cat would be easy peasy. She transformed that three-hundred-pound demon into a little fluffball like a pro, but she'd never gotten the chance to try undoing that spell. "Mike, I'm not—"

"Shh..." He took both her hands in his. "Don't even say it. I *know* you can do this. Confidence is key."

She nodded. "Confidence is key." Real confidence. Not the fake it 'til you make it kind she'd fabricated in the past. She *could* do this. She had to.

"Your time starts now."

"I love you, Mike," she whispered as she slipped from his grasp.

"I love you too." He straightened his spine and winked. "I'm ready."

With a deep inhale, she opened her channel to the goddess, whispered the incantation, and turned Mike into a sleek black cat. He sat on his haunches, his red eyes trained on her as Rosemary transformed Amarillo into a brown tabby. Crimson had performed the spell faster, but could she change Mike back?

Her stomach churned like she'd eaten a dozen bean burritos and washed them down with expired milk. She swallowed the dryness from her mouth, opened her channel to the goddess full blast, and with as much confidence in her voice as she could muster, she chanted the undoing spell she'd never gotten right before.

The air around Mike's fur shimmered, and he let out garbled meow as his shape wavered. Crimson blinked, holding her breath as his form elongated. *Please work. Please work.* The sparkling magic around him dissipated, and she looked into the deep brown eyes of her demon.

"That was fun." Red flashed in his irises as he grinned. "I knew you could do it."

She flung her arms around his neck and squeezed him tight. "Oh, thank the goddess, thank the Devil, thank *you.*"

His chest rumbled with his laugh. "This gives me an idea for a little role-playing game tonight."

"Oh, no." She shook her head adamantly. "No spells in the bedroom."

"Okay." He brushed a curl from her forehead. "We'll be making plenty of magic on our own anyway."

"That we will."

"Who won?" Rosemary shooed Amarillo back to her seat. "She was faster on that one, but I beat her on everything else. I know I did."

Laila closed her eyes, lifting her arms as magic sparkled on her fingertips. "The name of the high priestess of the New Orleans Coven of Witches." The air above her shimmered, and a name appeared in golden glitter. *Crimson.*

Her head spun, and as she swayed, Mike held her close to his body, steadying her.

"What?" Rosemary gasped. "That can't be right. She's incompetent. She's a fool. She's—"

"Crimson has won the challenge," Laila said.

Every witch in attendance looked at Crimson and said,

"So mote it be." A few gasps sounded from the audience, and Sophie let out a "Woot!"

"No. No! This isn't right." Rosemary held up her hands, backing away from Crimson. "She's in cahoots with a demon. She had help from the Devil himself. You don't want her as your leader. You want me. Me!"

A witch in a mauve robe handed Laila the massive volume of coven law, and she opened it, nodding solemnly. "The new high priestess will now bind the magic of the loser before the exile begins."

"Actually…" Crimson checked the time. Exactly three o'clock. "Someone has an offer for you that might be a better deal."

A hole ripped in the air next to Crimson, and she and Mike moved back as Satan stepped through the portal. He wore a deep red Prada suit with an onyx tie and polished red shoes. A collective gasp sounded from the audience, and Rosemary's eyes widened when the Devil strolled toward her, a devious grin curving his lips.

"Is this the one you told me about?" he asked over his shoulder.

"She's the one," Crimson replied.

"What's your name?" Satan raked his gaze up and down her squat form.

"Rosemary Duncan." She straightened to her full height, which wasn't much, and inclined her chin. "You've got some nerve showing up here after my repeated requests for help. Some Devil you are."

Satan laughed. "A sharp tongue and she shows no fear. Rosemary Duncan. Oh, yes. I remember seeing your name on my list. Your request came in while I was on vacation with a banshee. My own personal hell, if you're inclined to ask. The woman wouldn't stop screaming. I won't be doing that again."

"You could have sent an advocate," she retorted. "What happened to *no rest for the wicked*?"

The Devil glanced at Mike. "My best advocate was busy exploring another witch, I'm afraid. All requests were frozen as I attended to the whims of a woman who would never understand me. I'm afraid my slip in judgment has caused a world of trouble for all of you, and for that, I am deeply...amused. This ordeal has been sincerely entertaining, but I must get back to work. I'm down one advocate, and I have a slew of souls to process, which is why I'm going to make you an offer."

He walked a slow circle around Rosemary, nodding. "Yes, she'll do fine." He stopped in front of her. "I need a new personal assistant. You'll help me process souls and assign them to the appropriate levels of the underworld."

"You want me to live in hell and be your assistant?" Rosemary's expression was incredulous.

"You'll get to help me torture wicked souls. It'll be so much fun." He held out his hands, palms up. "Or you can accept your punishment from the coven and live the rest of your measly life as a human. What do you say? Personal Assistant to the Prince of the Underworld is quite a title."

"*Red* will take me under," Rosemary whispered. "Not Crimson." She swallowed hard and stuck out her hand. "You have a deal."

Satan glanced over his shoulder. "Michael, would you like to seal this one, for old time's sake?"

Mike shoved his hands into his pockets. "I'm good."

The Devil sighed. "Very well." He shook Rosemary's hand, opening a portal with his other and dragging her through.

As the gateway snapped shut, stunned silence filled the room. The Devil had made an appearance in the coven house. Rosemary was gone. Crimson had won the challenge, and that was probably the most surprising of all.

She looked at Laila, expecting her to speak, but her friend's reassuring smile reminded her that *she* was now the high priestess, and she needed to address her coven. "So, that was wild, wasn't it?"

A nervous giggle escaped her lips, and the energy in the room lightened. She cleared her throat. "This is Mike, my boyfriend, and it's true that he's a recovering Devil's advocate. I do know Satan, but only because I had to travel to hell to get Mike back. Oh, and my mom was there too. Anyway, I know the goddess proclaimed me high priestess, but I don't want to force myself on you the way someone *else* did."

Some of the witches whispered to each other, but Crimson couldn't make out their words. She stepped forward, filling her voice with confidence. "I'd like to call a vote. My magic works properly now, which I believe I've just proven, but if you don't want me as your leader, I will step down and allow you to elect the priestess of your choice." She looked at Laila. "We can do it blindly. Have everyone write down their decision."

Laila smiled. "I don't think we need to."

"Anyone willing to take on Rosemary will be a fantastic leader." Fern rose and stepped onto the floor. "I move we keep Crimson as high priestess."

Willow stood. "The goddess deemed it be, and that's good enough for me."

"And me," Agatha said.

One by one, every witch in the coven stood, nodding

her agreement to keep Crimson on as high priestess, and her heart swelled with joy and gratitude.

"I know my vote doesn't count," Sophie said, "but y'all are lucky to have Crimson. She's the best witch I've ever met."

Crimson smiled. "Well, then, I promise to be the best high priestess I can be until I'm too old to lead you."

Mike cleared his throat. "About that... Anyone who makes it to hell and back with their body intact is granted immortality. It's a clause in all Satan's contracts that he doesn't tell anyone about."

"Then I guess I'll be the best high priestess I can be until y'all get tired of me or I retire, whichever comes first." She slinked toward Mike, linking her fingers behind his neck. "But you, sir, are stuck with me for all eternity."

As he grinned, his eyes flashed red. "*That's* my greatest desire."

Crescent City Wolf Pack Series

Werewolves Only

Beneath a Blue Moon

Bound by Blood

A Deal with Death

A Song to Remember

Crescent City Ghost Tours Series

Love & Ghosts

Love & Omens

New Orleans Nocturnes Series

License to Bite

Shift Happens

Life's a Witch

Spirit Chasers Series

To Catch a Spirit

To Stop a Shadow

To Free a Phantom

ABOUT THE AUTHOR

Carrie Pulkinen is a paranormal romance author who has always been fascinated with things that go bump in the night. Of course, when you grow up next door to a cemetery, the dead (and the undead) are hard to ignore. Pair that with her passion for writing and her love of a good happily-ever-after, and becoming a paranormal romance author seems like the only logical career choice.

Before she decided to turn her love of the written word into a career, Carrie spent the first part of her professional life as a high school journalism and yearbook teacher. She loves good chocolate and bad puns, and in her free time, she likes to read, drink wine, and travel with her family.

Connect with Carrie online:
www.CarriePulkinen.com

Printed in Poland
by Amazon Fulfillment
Poland Sp. z o.o., Wrocław

58896924R00101